MURDER IN THE EARLY HOURS

BLYTHE BAKER

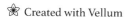 Created with Vellum

When Alice Beckingham finally uncovers the truth about her brother's death, she must set off for New York City in search of the powerful criminal responsible. An unexpected family reunion pulls her cousin Rose and the famous detective Achilles Prideaux into the case, even if Rose seems mysteriously reluctant to be involved.

Alice's search for her brother's killer will lead her from the streets of the city to the highest echelons of New York society as she closes in on the shadowy villain.

With the murder of an informant destroying Alice's best hopes of cornering her enemy, will she ever find justice for her family? Or will the painful mystery that has tormented her for years go forever unsolved?

1

When I rounded the corner at the end of the block from my family's home, I expected to see a tall, lean figure standing there. Probably shrouded in shadows as he always was, as though they trailed around with him, ready to shield him from view at a moment's notice.

Instead, the corner was empty.

I stopped, panicked for a moment, and wondered if I should continue walking and make a loop around the block. Except, I didn't want to walk past my house again. I'd slipped out without anyone noticing, and if Mama was still in the sitting room, she might witness me pass and come to see where I was going.

She would not be pleased when she saw Sherborne Sharp waiting for me at the corner.

Though, since he hadn't yet arrived, I wondered if he ever would. He had left hastily enough the night before, leaving me with nothing but a slip of paper that said to meet him here at this exact time. Yet, where was he? He'd never been late before.

"I'm here, I'm here."

I turned and saw Sherborne walking towards me across the street. His dark hair was almost hidden beneath a gray hat that matched his gray pinstripe suit. The jacket hung loosely around him, and the hollows along his cheeks looked more pronounced than usual. Had he lost weight? The dark vest fit him tightly enough that I couldn't tell. It could have easily been that the jacket was secondhand and not fitted to his specifications. Either way, I reminded myself, his weight did not concern me. Sherborne had information, and I wanted to hear it.

"I announced myself lest I startle you as I did last night," he said, mounting the curb with something like amusement playing on his lips. "The threat of being hit with your purse has frightened me into being more cautious, though you don't seem to be carrying a bag today. Lucky me."

"Lucky indeed," I grumbled.

He tilted his head to the side and removed his hat, running a hand through his hair to ensure it wasn't flattened. For all of his swagger, he cared about appearances and opinions, including mine. "Are you so set on being cross with me? I thought we'd resolved to be friends last night."

He seemed to stutter over the word "friends," and my mind, too, stuck on it. Since I'd found Sherborne Sharp standing amongst my mother's belongings with the intent of stealing them so many weeks ago, it was hard to imagine our relationship had evolved to anything beyond thief and victim. Yet, here we were, meeting on a corner to exchange secrets. Or rather, exchange money for secrets.

Sherborne had never named his price for the detective work I sent him out on, but I stashed a bit of money in my skirt pocket before leaving the house, anyway.

"I am set on being cross so long as you are set on teasing me. Behave and perhaps my demeanor will improve."

His eyes sparkled even as he nodded his head in reverent understanding. "Is this a good place to talk or are you worried about your mother seeing us together?"

The question made my cheeks warm. First, because the way his voice dropped when he said the word 'together' made it sound like we were meeting for purposes beyond a professional conversation. Second, because it implied I was a child still under the thumb of my mother. The fact that I'd been too afraid to pass by the sitting room window a second time lest she see me further proved his point and left me feeling even more cross.

"I am free to meet with whomever I choose, though my mother's feelings about me meeting a man who nearly stole from her collection of jewelry could make my life more difficult. If we are meeting in secret, it is your fault, not mine."

He frowned. "You told your mother? I thought..."

His voice trailed off, and he sounded truly shaken for the first time.

"I did not," I assured him immediately, feeling guilty for holding the situation over his head. He had settled his debts and earned my trust long ago.

"Then there is no reason we can't meet in your home

like civilized people," he said, tipping his head in the direction of the house and taking a step forward. "I'd love to see your mother again. Shall we?"

He'd called my bluff and made me doubt my trust in him. If he wished for our conversation to be more civil, he was doing a bad job of showing it.

I grabbed his arm to stop him and planted my feet firmly on the cement. "Please tell me what you've uncovered. I don't have time for whatever game you are playing."

Sherborne's jaw clenched. "I do not think it is I who is playing games."

"What is that supposed to mean?" I let go of his arm and took a step away. "You are the one who asked me to meet you here. Did you have a reason for that or—?"

"Of course," he said coldly. "Why else would I want to meet with you if not for business?"

There was sarcasm in his voice, but I couldn't understand where it came from. If either one of us was allowed to be annoyed, it was me. Sherborne had brought me from my home with the promise of information and, instead, insulted my independence.

"You are maddening," I mumbled.

He leaned forward, a wisp of dark hair falling across his forehead. "Believe me, the feeling is mutual."

A woman passed by with a small dog on a long leash and smiled in our direction. Sherborne tipped his hat, but I just looked away. I wasn't in a very friendly mood.

"Do not worry. She didn't look closely enough to recognize you even if she does know your mother," he said. "Your reputation is safe."

The thought hadn't even crossed my mind, but I

didn't say so. "What information do you have for me?"

"You wanted me to look into the existence of this person called The Chess Master and his fate, and I have," Sherborne said, shrugging his hands into his pockets and staring off to the left, his eyes focused on something far beyond the stone house in front of him. "The information available is limited unless you are willing to risk your life by involving yourself with the city's darkest criminals. Still, I was able to track down people who had heard of him, and they all said the same thing: The Chess Master fell from a bridge into the river Thames."

Was this good news? I couldn't tell. I let the information settle inside of me, trying to gauge what I'd hoped for, but where I expected to find emotion, there was nothing.

If the Chess Master had been responsible for Edward's death, wasn't it a fitting end for him to die in a gruesome way? The world certainly must be better for it. Still, I did not feel relief or closure. I felt...nothing.

"Is that a satisfactory ending for you?" Sherborne asked.

My brows drew together, and even before I answered aloud, Sherborne sighed. "I assumed as much. Which is why I found a past partner of The Chess Master who would speak with me."

My head snapped up. "You said that would be risking your life."

"I did, didn't I?" His mouth pulled into a half-smile, and the emptiness in my chest filled with warmth.

"Who did you speak with? What did they say?"

"The man I found is a single cog in a large machine The Chess Master utilized for smuggling art and other stolen goods out of the country. He was only willing to talk to me because his position is so insignificant, no one believes him to have any information of true value."

The man hardly seemed worth risking his life over, yet I was hanging on Sherborne's every word. "What does he do?"

"He is a deck hand on a steamer boat," Sherborne said. "*The* steamer boat it is rumored The Chess Master swam to after falling from the bridge that night two years ago."

Sherborne's smile faded, and I stared at him, waiting for the information to settle over me. When it finally did, I let out a slow breath. "So, he is alive?"

"If rumors can be trusted." Sherborne shrugged.

"What do you think?"

He tipped his head back and once again focused his dark eyes across the street. "You care about my opinion?"

"You spoke with the man personally, yes? I'd like to know what you thought of him. Whether you gauge him to be reliable." Also, I still didn't know how to react. It seemed easier to let Sherborne do the thinking while I tried to gather my thoughts.

Sherborne sighed and stepped forward, lowering his head and his voice. "The man was half-drunk when I spoke to him. I'm not sure he would have taken any of my questions had he been sober. On one hand, that seems to work in favor of him telling the truth. Drink often brings out the truths we try to hide away. However, it could also mean that he was simply loose enough to entertain the wild rumors he had heard. Rumors are certain to surround a criminal of this stature. The man would not say with any certainty whether he had seen The Chess

Master board the ship that night. He only said other men from the ship that night whispered that the boat took the Chess Master back to shore where they later heard he boarded a ship set for New York."

I nodded. "Those are all possibilities."

Sherborne reached for my hand, and I did not pull it away. His fingers were long and thin and warm, and I watched as his thumb swept over my knuckles. "If you truly want to know what I think, I must tell you I do not know what to think. The man could be dead or alive, in London or living abroad. The only thing I do know is that this is not a man you should involve yourself with, Alice."

He spoke my name slowly but with force, punctuating the end of his sentence with it. He shook his head. "If he is alive, he heads an international criminal organization and is still feared enough that men will only speak about him in hushed tones. He is not a jealous actor or a disgruntled maid, like the villains you've encountered in the past. This man has serious power, and I would advise you not to tangle with him."

"Thank you," I said, sliding my hand away from his and pulling the bundle of money from my pocket. "We never discussed a price, but I have more than enough here to cover your troubles."

Sherborne stepped back like he had been physically pushed. "My price? Alice—"

"Money conversations are always uncomfortable, but we agreed that you have more than made up for the unfortunate incident with my mother's jewelry. I will not blackmail you for information, so if you are going to work for me, then I would like to make sure you are compensated."

"Work for you?" Sherborne removed his hat and ruffled his dark hair. He twisted the hat in his hands before pushing it back on his head roughly. "I did not seek out this information for money. I do not want to take anything from you."

"Then why?" I lowered the money to my side, unsure if I should press the matter or put it away. "Why would you risk your life for nothing?"

"Because it wasn't for nothing." The words rushed out of him hotly, and he shook his head. "I did it so you wouldn't have to, Alice. I did it because I didn't want you endangering yourself by looking into the matter on your own. I did it to keep you safe."

Emotion warred in my chest. Gratitude swelled and then was beaten down by pride. The waves sloshed inside of me, tempestuous, as I tried to understand his meaning.

"I'm not a child, Mr. Sharp. I—"

"Mr. Sharp." He let out a humorless chuckle and looked up at me, his eyes shining with passion. "We are friends, Alice. You know my name."

"I'm not a child, Sherborne," I corrected, emphasizing his name. "I appreciate your assistance and am happy to pay you for your trouble, but I do not require a handler. I am a woman perfectly capable of looking after herself."

How many times had I said the same thing to my parents? To Catherine? Even to my cousin, Rose? No matter how I proved myself competent and capable, no one seemed able to view me as anything other than a child. Sherborne has always been a friend in my eyes, despite our playful bickering, and I thought out of everyone I knew, he would be the one to see me as an equal. Yet, I had just learned the truth. He only assisted me for fear of what would happen to me if he didn't. It was insulting.

"This isn't a matter of capability. It is a matter of sanity," Sherborne said. "To go after The Chess Master for information beyond what I've discovered would be dangerous. You would be putting your life at risk."

My brother had paid with his life for getting involved with The Chess Master. I knew the price better than anyone. Certainly better than Sherborne.

"If you are a friend, then you'll allow me to make up my own mind on the matter," I said, not betraying to him that a plan was already forming in the back of my mind. I tucked the money in my pocket and lifted a hand in a wave. "Thank you again for your time, Sherborne. I suspect I will see you again soon."

Sherborne grabbed my hand suddenly, holding me in place. "I can only count myself a true friend if I am honest and speak my mind. So, I must tell you, I do not think you should go after this man. You've had luck with smaller cases, but this is beyond either of our expertise. You are dabbling in things you do not understand, and I wish you would steer away from it entirely. Please."

His fingers loosened around mine but still held, the pressure warm and pleading, matching the tone of his voice.

I felt the sincerity in his words, but my pride prickled at being told what I ought and ought not to do. I pulled my hand away and straightened my skirt.

"You've said more than enough on the subject already, so it is my turn to be honest and ask you to refrain from saying any more."

"Alice," he breathed, trying to interrupt me.

I continued as though he had said nothing. "I have reasons you do not understand for my interest in The Chess Master, and for that reason I will continue without any further assistance from you."

"Alice, you are being foolish." Sherborne raised his voice and fisted his hands at his side.

"And you're a coward." The words were out before I could stop them. I wanted to reel them back in when Sherborne's lips pressed together in obvious hurt and shock, but it was too late. I set my brow.

His shoulders dropped, and he backed away from me, stepping down into the gutter. He raised his hands in resignation. "Only a true friend would dare be so honest." His words were acid. Sarcastic and biting. "Goodbye, Alice."

I wanted to call after him as he turned to leave, hoping to see a hint of his usual smirk, any sign that we were parting as friends, but Sherborne did not look back as he crossed the street and walked down the block. I watched his retreating form until he was out of sight.

Sherborne had hoped to sate my interest in the criminal mastermind and end my searching, but it was too late for that. Sherborne had warned me not to entangle myself with The Chess Master, but I had already tangled with him. Or rather, The Chess Master had tangled with me.

The moment he arranged my brother's murder, The Chess Master put himself on a course that would one day converge with mine. The extent of that convergence remained to be seen, but Sherborne's findings were not the end of my journey. They were merely the beginning.

2

I drafted my telegram to my Aunt Sarah as soon as I got back to my room after my meeting with Sherborne, informing her of my desire to visit her in New York City, and had it sent late that afternoon.

When Catherine, Rose, and I had left the city last to attend Catherine and Charles' wedding in Somerset, Aunt Sarah had all but begged us to return often. With no children of her own and her husband long dead, she said her house felt too large. She adored having company, and I knew she would be thrilled to have me as her extended guest.

Mama and Papa, however, were less thrilled.

"Wait until we can secure an escort for you," Mama said. "It wouldn't be proper for you to travel alone. You, a beautiful, wealthy girl. You need someone to assist you."

"*Woman*," I corrected her, though she was too busy appealing to my father to hear me.

"Tell Alice it wouldn't be proper, James."

My father lowered his newspaper and studied me, his

shrewd eyes taking in my determined expression and posture. "Are you set upon this trip, Alice?"

I nodded. "Entirely."

"We won't hear the end of it if you are forced to remain at home?"

"I don't believe it is within your power to force me," I said. "You would need to tie me up."

He sighed and flicked his eyes back to his paper. "Sorry, my dear, but I believe Alice is intent upon this trip."

"You can't be serious," Mama said. "You are her father. Force her to stay."

He shrugged as though it was useless, and I jumped forward and clutched my mother's hand between my own. "Aunt Sarah wrote only a few weeks ago that she misses me and wishes I would visit. It would be lovely to see her again and shop in the stores there. I can bring you back all the latest fashions."

"I don't care about those things," Mama said, laying a hand over my cheek. "I care about you."

"Then let me go," I said sincerely.

In the end, she did not really have a say in the matter anyway, but she agreed the trip could be beneficial. She worried about her sister living alone in that big house and wanted someone to check on her health and wellbeing. My mother had been trying to get Aunt Sarah to move to London for years, but my aunt enjoyed her friends and social life in America too much to leave. I knew my mother partially hoped I would find Aunt Sarah in desperate need of caring for and bring her back to London on the ship with me. I, however, knew my aunt well enough to know that would not be the case. Aunt Sarah was the most capable person I had ever met.

Her response arrived just after breakfast the next day: *Your room is ready. Love, Aunt Sarah.*

I spent several days preparing for the trip, allowing my mother to take me shopping and buy things I certainly did not need. I reminded her several times that I could buy whatever I needed in New York, but she insisted I needed extra under things and stockings and a new hat.

"If you are going to be on the ship alone, I want you to look respectable."

"Is my appearance now not respectable?" I asked, looking down at my wool coat, blue cotton dress, and T-strap heels.

"You know that is not what I mean." She never did clarify exactly what she meant, even as she bought me a second hat and another dress to wear to dinner on the ship.

As we shopped, I looked for Sherborne.

I cannot say exactly why, as he would never have been seen in some of the shops my mother and I ventured into. Yet, I wanted to see him. We had left things on bad terms. I'd tried to write him a letter, but I couldn't find the words. My apologies felt thin and false, especially since I had no intention of heeding the advice I had so harshly thrown back in his face, and I did not want him to know about my plans.

If I told him I was leaving for New York, I was afraid he would try to stop me. His threats that day on the corner to go and speak with my parents had been in jest, but if he thought I was really in danger, would he go to them? Would he tell them of my intentions to find answers about my brother's murder?

My mother and father were under the impression my visit to Aunt Sarah was nothing more than a sudden desire to see New York again and socialize with new people. Papa, who disliked most of my friends in London, thought it would be a good opportunity to make more serious acquaintances, and I knew Mama hoped I would find a man to marry just as Catherine had.

Even with those reasons, they were barely on board with the trip. If they knew the real reason I was going there—that I could be putting myself in harm's way— they really would have tied me up in my room to keep me from going. They'd already lost one child to a life of crime and murder, and they would not take kindly to a second child becoming involved in that world.

So, I didn't say anything to Sherborne. I simply looked for him wherever we went.

On the morning my parents took me to the dock to say goodbye, Papa carried my trunk and Mama tied a scarf around my neck.

"It will be colder at sea than on land. Do you have warm enough clothes?" she asked.

"Even if I don't, it is too late to do anything about it now," I said.

She waved my reasoning away. "We could always buy you another ticket. You do not have to go today. I don't think I could sleep easily if I thought you were cold and shivering in the middle of the Atlantic."

I grabbed her hand and squeezed. "I've been on a ship before, Mama. Several times."

"But never alone." Her eyes sparkled, and I could see

the fear there.

My parents did a good job of looking cheerful. In the weeks and months after Edward's crime and eventual murder in prison, they fell apart. Understandably so. Our house was dark and vacant of its usual warmth and joy.

Once they'd had their time of mourning, however, Mama and Papa locked those feelings away and did their best to move forward. They laughed and joked and only grew somber when Edward was the specific topic of conversation.

I could see the scar of that time in my mother's eyes, though. The wound that kind of pain had left on her mind and heart. She was terrified of something happening to another of her children.

I pulled her into a hug, patting her back and pressing my cheek against hers. "I will be fine, Mama. I'll send word the moment my feet hit solid ground."

Papa smiled at me over her shoulder and then tipped his head towards the ship. "You had better go before they pull in the gangplank and you have no choice."

My mother held me tighter. "That is a good idea. I'll hold you here until the ship is gone."

I laughed and extracted myself from her hold. "Aunt Sarah will take good care of me, and I'll take care of her, too."

"Send my love to my sister," Mama said, patting my hand fondly. "And be careful, Alice. Make friends with someone trustworthy on the boat. Make sure someone knows where you are."

I promised her I would take every precaution and be incredibly careful, and after several more tight hugs during which I thought my mother really might hold me hostage in her arms, I finally said my goodbyes and boarded the ship.

A young couple walked up the ramp behind me. The man was carrying the luggage while the woman laughed at some joke he'd made. As we all reached the top of the ramp, my trunk got caught on the corner of the opening. Before a crew member could come assist me, the man jumped forward and lifted the back end with his foot, helping the trunk over the threshold.

"Carrying my luggage and this young lady's," the woman with him teased. "Why did this ship even bother hiring crew?"

I laughed at her joke and thanked the man for his assistance. Once I made it onto the deck, I stopped to readjust my grip and watched as the couple walked down the deck in the direction of their quarters.

I didn't mind travelling alone, but watching the two of them smile and laugh with one another, I wondered what it would be like to have a male friend of my own to carry my luggage and laugh with.

Sherborne Sharp's face came to my mind unbidden.

Rarely ever did we laugh and joke. Our relationship, if it could be described as such, revolved around constant teasing and bickering. We could barely work together in a business sense, so I would hate to see the devastation that would come if we attempted to be trapped together on a ship.

Still, I wondered.

As I got to my cabin, I brushed the thought of Sherborne away and accepted the reality. I was alone on a ship headed for America. Headed for The Chess Master. That was where my attention needed to be right now.

3

F inding my Aunt Sarah was easy in the crowd. I simply had to look for my mother.

The two women had always looked alike, but their similarities increased with age. They had the same pointed chins and wide, smiling mouths. Their eyes crinkled at the corners, and they each stood a head shorter than most people around them.

For that reason, I identified my aunt by the frantic waving of her arm rather than by her face.

As I scanned the dock, searching for my relations and my ride, I saw a thin arm with a jangle of bracelets stacked around the wrist arcing quickly through the air, and I smiled.

When I reached my aunt, she grinned and pulled me into a tight hug.

"You are taller," she said, holding me by the elbows and stepping back. "You've grown since I saw you last. How dare you? Tall and beautiful. It is hardly fair."

"I'm only tall compared to you and Mama," I teased,

earning myself a narrow-eyed grin. "You did not need to come to the docks, Aunt Sarah. I could have met you at the house."

This was true, though I'd known all along Aunt Sarah would be waiting for me. She had enough money to hire one-hundred servants, so she easily could have sent a driver to fetch me, but Aunt Sarah seemed to be the only person who didn't realize how incredibly wealthy she was. When it was possible for her to do something herself, she would.

She waved my words away dismissively. "I would never let you walk into my city on your own. It wouldn't be right. Do you have all of your things?"

I looked down at my single trunk and nodded. Aunt Sarah seemed pleased that I had travelled with so little and led me to where her driver was waiting for us both.

The argument could be made that New York City and London were similar—both large cities with large, diverse populations—certainly similar enough that a Londoner wouldn't come to New York City and be awed by it.

Yet, I was awed.

Even with it being my second time in New York, as we drove along, I couldn't help but cling to the door and stare at the buildings and people we passed. Everything seemed so new and sparkling. Part of that was probably because of the sunshine.

London seemed to exist in a near-constant haze of overcast skies and morning fog, but the sunlight cut straight through the clouds and shone upon New York in all of its glory.

Aunt Sarah pointed out some of her favorite shops

and restaurants as we neared the part of the city where she lived, and we made unofficial plans to visit all of them. Neither of us had spoken about how long I would be staying in New York, but Aunt Sarah seemed content to make plans as though I was moving there permanently. I didn't mind this in the slightest.

Then, the buildings and businesses gave way to residential neighborhoods and towering stone homes with lush green gardens and imposing fences. This was the part of the city that reminded me most of home. It looked like the very neighborhood I had grown up in, though the stones looked newer.

At home, facades were covered by dense layers of dirt and moss and age that had to be cleaned regularly due to the damp conditions. In New York, however, everything looked as though it had just been built. Based upon some of the scaffolding I saw around a few of the homes, I wouldn't have been surprised if that was the case, after all.

The homes grew more luxurious as we drove further down Fifth Avenue, and then, as Central Park rose on one side of us, Aunt Sarah's house took shape up ahead.

In a long line of brick and stone mansions, her house managed to set itself apart.

It stood on a corner lot with two faces, each unique. The first facing the park across the street, the other a wide road and the inferior mansion opposite.

The park side was of shining white stone with large gaping windows that I knew from experience allowed decadent views of city and nature coexisting just across the road. The strips of stone between windows were so narrow it seemed impossible for the house to remain standing, yet it did.

The roof was dark in contrast with the white stone and covered in chimneys, towers, and parapets, hinting at the elaborate design of the interior of the house even as they made it difficult to focus on the design of the exterior.

Then, just when it seemed the house could not be more lovely, the driver turned the corner and revealed the gothic arches and spires of the second side. They were thin and pointed, drawing the eye up and to the blue sky beyond as though the house itself was a doorway to the heavens.

Even after a life spent surrounded by wealth and luxury, Aunt Sarah's home took my breath away.

"Are you coming, Alice?" Aunt Sarah teased, after the car had pulled to a stop and she had hopped out. She stood on the sidewalk just behind the driver while I stared up, mouth open at the house.

The driver told me not to worry about my things, and I let my aunt lead me up the stone steps to her front door and into the massive foyer.

Marble stretched in every direction, broken up only by thickly woven rugs and gold trim around the doorways, floors, and ceilings. Mural-covered domes capped many of the main rooms and the furniture was all velvet and leather and satin.

I was still admiring the mural above the entryway, a scene of a partially clothed woman drinking from a crystal pond while deer and other forest wildlife looked on, when I heard the distinct clearing of a throat and looked to my left to see my cousin Rose standing in front of me.

It had been some time since I'd seen her face-to-face, and it took me several stunned seconds to react at all. When I did, I blinked and then stepped forward to pull her into a hug.

Rose's blonde hair was cropped short, her curls pinned down across her forehead and behind her ears with a lace headband. Her dress was less extravagant than those I was accustomed to, made of simple cotton and hanging down to her knees in straight lines. I assumed it was more in the style of Nellie Dennet than Rose Beckingham. Though only myself, my sister Catherine, my parents, and Achilles Prideaux knew the true identity of "Rose," being unburdened to her closest kin had given my cousin the opportunity to blend her two identities into one that made her more comfortable.

"What are you doing here?" I whispered against her ear, still unsure how I could be hugging her. "You are meant to be in San Francisco."

"Actually, I'm meant to be here," she said with a laugh. "Achilles and I had to come this way for work sooner or later, so when Aunt Sarah sent word you would be visiting, we decided sooner would be better."

"No one told me," I said, giving my aunt a firm expression. "I was not prepared."

Aunt Sarah shrugged. "I've found one only really needs to be prepared for bad news. I knew Rose's visit would be good news, so I said nothing."

"It is good news," I agreed, hugging my cousin again. "The best news. I'm so happy to see you."

Rose studied my face in the way that was her habit,

examining every hair and pore. She liked to look at everything before her carefully and thoroughly, including me. I allowed her thirty seconds of inspection before I pulled away and walked past her into the sitting room.

I sighed as I lowered myself onto the velvet loveseat. "I was so exhausted walking off the ship that I assumed I would come straight here and sleep all day, but suddenly, I'm wide awake."

"Achilles and I plan to be in the city for a while, so please do not stay up on my account."

"Yes," Aunt Sarah echoed. "Rest, Alice, if you'd like. I will see to it that your room is completely ready and then you are more than welcome to sleep the day away. Inform me of your schedule, and I'll match it. We can live like owls while you are here if you'd like. Being nocturnal sounds like an adventure to me."

Aunt Sarah hurried away in a bustle of fabrics and soft heel taps across the floor, leaving Rose and myself alone for the first time. I felt the first hint of tension in the air. My own detective instincts, though likely inferior to my cousin's, prickled.

Aside from her less extravagant clothes, Rose looked the same as she had the last time I'd seen her. Same hairstyle and smooth complexion.

The only thing there was to suggest all was not well was the way Rose wrung her hands as she sat down on the sofa across from me. I could see she still wore the wedding ring Achilles had given her, so even though I had not seen him yet, I had good reason to suspect he would make his appearance known soon.

So, there was nothing out of place to alert me ahead of time to my cousin's abrupt and startling change of conversation.

"I know you are here in search of The Chess Master," Rose said quietly.

If I'd been prepared for anyone to guess my reason for being in the city, I would have prepared a lie. As it was, however, I had no reason to think anyone would be suspicious, so I had nothing prepared.

I stared at Rose, blinking and searching for words that would not come.

"You are not denying it because you can't," Rose said, folding her nervous hands in her lap. "You wrote to me about him, and I told you the matter was closed, yet you are still searching. Why?"

"How do you know?" I asked, returning her question with a question of my own. "Who told you? Was it Sherborne?"

I had no idea how my friend would have come into contact with my cousin living in San Francisco, but there was very little I did not think Sherborne capable of. If he set his mind to protecting me from The Chess Master, I had every faith he could figure out who to contact and how to find them.

Rose frowned. "Who is Sherborne?"

I shook my head, chiding myself for revealing more information than necessary. "No one. How did you know why I came here?"

Rose tilted her head to the side and raised a blonde brow at me. "I make a living out of solving the most difficult cases in the world. I am sorry, Alice, but your motives were not difficult to uncover."

My cheeks warmed.

I felt like a little girl caught with my hand in the sweets tin.

Thankfully, Achilles Prideaux chose that moment to make his appearance. For a second after the tall, thin Frenchman walked through the door, I thought they were going to gang up on me, but then I saw Rose's face fall into disappointment. Whatever she was about to tell me, she didn't want to say it in front of her husband.

I was relieved, but also disappointed. I never could handle not being let in on a secret.

"Alice," Achilles said warmly, though he made no move to hug me or even so much as shake my hand. He folded his hands over the crook of his cane and hovered in the doorway. "It is so nice to see you. Rose was thrilled our trips could overlap like this."

"Oh, yes," I said, looking back and forth at them both. "What are you in New York for, anyway? Rose said it was business but nothing else."

"There isn't much to tell," Achilles said, a sudden sharpness entering his voice. "Just another boring case. Nothing interesting."

I had not known a single case Achilles and Rose took on to ever be boring. They were often tasked with uncovering international assassins, solving high-profile murders, and tracking down stolen items worth two of Aunt Sarah's Fifth Avenue mansion. However, I also knew Achilles would not reveal anything to me he did not want to reveal, so I didn't ask any more questions.

"I only came down for a bit of tea," he said. "Should we all take some in the sunroom?"

Rose looked close to refusing his offer, but I stood to my feet and wrapped my arm through his before either of them could respond. Achilles looked momentarily stunned by my eagerness, but relaxed and escorted me to the sunroom on one side with his silently fuming wife on the other.

AUNT SARAH JOINED us for tea, and we spent most of the afternoon snacking on puddings and sipping tea, catching up. Our aunt spoke excitedly about the volunteer work she had been doing with her friends and local groups.

We talked well into the afternoon and by the time dinner arrived, I was full on sweets and the exhaustion I'd felt on the ship had returned.

"I think I will skip dinner and go to sleep early," I said, squeezing Aunt Sarah's hand before standing up and pushing in my chair. "I am liable to fall over at the table if I try to eat with you all."

They all bid me farewell, and I felt Rose's eyes in particular on me as I walked out of the room and up the polished wooden stairs to my room on the second floor.

The bed was made of solid wood with four intricately-carved posts and golden curtains hanging from them. The walls were a deep midnight blue with gold trim, but I hardly noticed the decoration as I folded my dress in the closet and exchanged it for a nightgown and robe from my trunk.

The time at sea had left me travel weary, and I had no doubt I would sleep the rest of the evening and through the night without difficulty.

I had just slipped into the plush bed and closed my

eyes when there was a knock at my door. Thinking it a servant coming to ensure I was comfortable, I invited them to come in, and was surprised to see Rose slip through the door and close it quietly behind her.

"You really were going to bed," she said. "I thought maybe you were just trying to get away from me."

I sat up, leaning back against the headboard. "Perhaps I had more than one motive."

Rose's mouth turned up in a smirk and she sat on the edge of my bed. "I know I probably seem dramatic. I barely let you walk through the door before I addressed why you are really here, but I don't want to delay and let something horrible happen."

"Nothing horrible will happen." I sighed. "I am always careful."

"There's no such thing where he is concerned," Rose said.

I did not need to ask who she was referring to.

Her tone was serious, yet she spoke about the man as though he was intimately familiar. If she had come here to squash my interest, she had failed.

"How do you know so much about him?"

Rose's shoulders heaved with a deep breath, and she stared down at her hands, knotted nervously in her lap. "You were the first person to welcome me into your family when you learned the truth of my identity, Alice. I've always appreciated your kindness and openness."

"You are my family," I said, leaning forward and laying a reassuring hand on her shoulder.

Rose smiled back at me and then returned her gaze to her hands. "I'm afraid, however, I have even more secrets that I haven't yet revealed. To anyone."

My heart clenched, but I tried to keep my expression neutral.

I had decided years ago that I would not turn my back on Rose. She had lied to us, but her choice had been a difficult one and, despite it all, I loved her dearly. Still, I worried she would say something that would change my opinion of her forever. I wanted my love for her to be unconditional, but was it really?

I supposed I was set to find out.

"I know about The Chess Master because I faced him. We met on a bridge, and I was there when he jumped over the side into the churning waters below."

I gasped. "Did he tell you anything about Edward? Is that why you tracked him down?"

"I didn't track him down," Rose said, shaking her head. "*He* found *me*."

I frowned, a wrinkle forming between my brows. This was all so shocking that I partly wondered whether I was actually dreaming. "Why would he do that?"

Rose looked back at me over her shoulder, her eyes heavy, mouth slanted down. "Because he is my brother."

Rose went on to tell me how her brother had disappeared from New York after their parents were killed while they were very young. She became an orphan and never knew what happened to him, until after the long chain of events that led to her being more or less adopted into my family. I knew some of the story already, but what I did not know was that The Chess Master reached out to Rose once she came to London.

"He taunted me," Rose said. "He warned me that someone would die during a holiday in Somerset with your family—the weekend your brother Edward killed

Catherine's first suitor. The Chess Master had me followed and monitored, and he was always one step ahead. Then, I caught up to him, and he revealed himself to me."

"And you pushed him," I said in a breath.

Rose shook her head again. "He jumped."

I pressed my hand to my chest, shocked. "Oh, Rose. I'm so sorry. That must have been a horrible thing to see. I can't even imagine."

"Remember why you are here?" Rose asked, looking up at me from beneath lowered brows.

The Chess Master survived and came to New York. I squeezed my eyes closed and took a steadying breath. "I nearly forgot. I got so wrapped up in your story."

"You heard the rumor that he survived," she continued. "I've heard that rumor, too."

"Is that why you are really in New York? Are you and Achilles here to find the Chess Master, too? Let me help you."

"Alice," Rose said, laying a hand over mine. "I am not looking for my brother. That part of my life is over now, and I am here to tell you the same. Let him be dead."

"But," I stammered, trying to understand. "He might be alive. Or do you think the rumors are just that, only rumors?"

Rose's shoulders tensed. "I always half-suspected my brother survived. For awhile, I thought it was paranoia, but the more I thought on it, the more I couldn't understand that ending for him. The Chess Master always had another plan. He prepared for every eventuality. When he walked into a room, he knew every exit and had a few secret exits prepared, as well. He would not have walked onto that bridge if the only way out was over the side."

I felt goosebumps form along my arms, and I folded them around my middle, fighting off a shiver. "Then how can you let him walk away? If he is as bad a criminal as people say, shouldn't you be working harder than anyone to find him?"

"I'm not certain he is alive. No one is. Besides, he is not worth it," Rose said simply.

Suddenly, my confusion gave way to anger. "He killed my brother."

Rose's expression softened, and her mouth twisted to one side. "I know, but you must admit that Edward willingly involved himself with dangerous people. What happened to him was horrible, but he killed someone, Alice. He was hardly innocent. It would be silly to put yourself in a dangerous position for the sake of simple vengeance."

"Justice is not vengeance," I snapped back. "Edward was serving his time for what he'd done. He did not deserve to die."

"Didn't he?" Rose asked. "He killed a man."

"And how many has The Chess Master killed?" I was sitting bolt upright in bed now. My face felt flushed with anger, and my hands shook. "If Edward deserved to die, then how much more does your brother deserve it?"

Rose flinched at the mention of her brother and turned away. "We can talk more tomorrow. You should rest."

"A good night's rest won't change my mind. You are reluctant to pursue The Chess Master because he is your brother. I'll understand your stance more if you are honest with me."

"That is not the situation at all," Rose said, standing up and spinning back towards the bed. "I understand what The Chess—what my brother has done. Believe me. That is why my concern is first and foremost for your safety. And mine."

"Then why would you let him walk free and give him the opportunity to hurt others?"

Rose opened her mouth to answer and then shook her head. "I think I should go. We should talk tomorrow."

I crossed my arms over my chest and stayed silent as she left. Rose was right on one point. She should go. But we would not be talking about this tomorrow.

4

Catherine sent me to New York with a list of her old friends I had to visit.

She and Mama had both insisted it would be incredibly rude of me to visit New York and not reach out to our family connections.

"They are not my connections," I'd argued. "I never met any of these people."

"Catherine said you did, and she sent a list with addresses. They are listed from most to least important," Mama had said.

I thought if my sister was capable of ranking her friends then they couldn't really all be that good of friends, but I'd decided it was better to hold my tongue and go along than to argue. I tucked the letter into my traveling trunk with no intention of calling on any of them.

Then, Rose had intruded on my trip and made staying in Aunt Sarah's house all day unbearable, so I dug the list from my trunk and sent word to the first name—

supposedly the most important person on the list: Helen Davis.

"Helen Davis is a lovely girl," Aunt Sarah said at breakfast. "She and Catherine were quite close, you recall."

"I don't, actually." I frowned. Catherine and I had come to Aunt Sarah's house after our brother's murder conviction and death, so it had been a trying time for me, anyway. Then, throwing in my near-obsession with finding an American boy to love, and it was no wonder I couldn't remember anyone else. Aunt Sarah said much the same thing.

"Helen Davis came over with her younger brother, Henry. Perhaps that is why you do not remember the woman." Aunt Sarah's lips were pressed together in a smug smile, and my face flushed.

"I recall Henry."

My aunt threw back her head and laughed. Rose managed a small chuckle, but she'd spent most of breakfast gazing at me over the rim of her teacup and smiling at Achilles to reassure him she was fine. Apparently, the detective sensed something was wrong because I could tell he kept squeezing his wife's knee under the table.

"I doubt Henry will be at your meeting with Helen today," Aunt Sarah said. "Last I heard, he was away at school, though I hardly keep up with the Davis family."

"I'd rather it just be me and Helen, anyway," I said, hoping my aunt would see I was far from the silly young girl I'd been the last time I'd visited. Truly, I had no interest in finding a suitor. The only man I cared to get to know was The Chess Master, and I suspected he would occupy most of my time.

"I could accompany you," Rose offered. "I remember Helen from when I visited. It might be less awkward if I go with you."

"I'm not even sure when I'll be seeing her. She might be busy today." That was true. If I remembered so little about Helen, it was possible she remembered equally little about me. She might not be in a rush to invite me over.

"I'm sure she'll get back to you as soon as possible. I can wait with you here."

I did my best to swallow down my annoyance and smiled. "I would hate for you to waste your day in such a tedious way."

Achilles frowned at his wife. "Besides, we have a meeting at the museum." He glanced around the table like he may have given too much away, but then turned his gaze back to Rose. "I told them we would arrive just after it opened."

Rose chewed on her lip, clearly torn, and then sighed. "Of course. I forgot."

I sent silent thanks to Achilles for saving me the trouble of having to refuse Rose's invitation. Truly, I didn't understand why she wanted to go with me in the first place. Unless, of course, she thought I was lying about meeting with Helen and instead planned to cavort around the city in search of The Chess Master.

Did she really expect me to just walk into an alleyway and reach out to the first criminals I encountered? The possibility made me angry that Rose could think so little of me.

Then, however, I had to face the fact that I had no idea how I would locate The Chess Master. Sherborne had been the one to reach out to the criminal element in London, but now I was on my own. I would have to do my own investigating if I wished to find out information. Especially since Rose would be of no help whatsoever.

Rose and Achilles left just after breakfast, and I spent the morning organizing my room with Aunt Sarah.

"Feel free to change the room in any way that will make you most comfortable. I never use this room, so I'm not attached to any of the décor. Tear it all down and buy new if you want. I have a line of credit with most shops, so just give them my name."

"The room is lovely," I told her as I unpacked the last dress from my trunk and hung it in the closet. Usually, a servant would have set to that task, but Aunt Sarah said they had more pressing matters to attend to than my wardrobe.

She was such a puzzling woman. On one hand, she could buy anything she desired and felt no concern at spending money frivolously, but on the other, she had her guests unpack their own clothes so as not to disturb the servants.

I didn't mind at all, but it was puzzling, nonetheless.

After my things were unpacked, I helped Aunt Sarah arrange the menu for a luncheon she planned to have with her friends. She invited me to join them, but just as she was asking, a note arrived for me, hand delivered by someone in Helen Davis' home staff.

Alice,

What a marvelous surprise to hear from you. I still correspond with Catherine frequently, but she did not mention you would be coming to visit. Of course, I would like to see you. Please come today for lunch if you can. If not, then for tea. I'll be home all day. Thrilled to catch up with you.

Helen

I changed from a simple skirt and blouse into a rose-colored linen dress and matching cloche hat more suitable for an afternoon gathering. Ivory detailing outlined the square neck and then travelled down the center of my dress to wrap around the dropped waist, giving the simple design a hint of elegance. I felt put together, indeed, as I approached the Davis' home—modest compared to the size and design detail of Aunt Sarah's—and knocked on the door.

A maid in a pale blue dress with a white apron answered the door and ushered me inside.

The house was narrow, but tall, with three levels if my assessment of the exterior could be trusted. A central hallway ran down the middle with the first-floor rooms branching off on either side. The wood floors, wallpaper, and rugs were all dark, but afternoon light came in through windows at the back of the house, casting out some of the gloom

"Miss Helen is waiting for you in the sitting room," the maid said, gesturing to the first door on the right just before the staircase.

I stepped inside and was instantly greeted by a high-pitched yelp.

The sitting room was much brighter than the hallway. Wide windows to my right let in a good amount of

sunlight that left me temporarily blinded in contrast with
the hallway. So, I did not realize who was standing in
front of me until I'd blinked several times, allowing my
vision to adjust, and saw a young woman with short
brown hair and a wide red smile in front of me.

I remembered her face even though I didn't think I
would.

"Helen," I said, grabbing the woman's extended hand
with both of mine. She clasped her hands around mine
until we were a tangle of hands and fingers. "Thank you
for having me over."

"Thank you for reaching out," she said, pulling me
towards the sofa. "I have missed Catherine fiercely since
she returned to England. How is she?"

"Good," I said, taking a seat near the fireplace. A
small fire burned there, though the room was already
warmer than comfortable due to the sunlight streaming
in. "She has a new baby daughter, and she and Charles
are as in love as ever."

"That's wonderful," Helen said.

She clapped her hands together, and the rattle of
jewelry on her wrist drew my attention from my own
awkwardness to Helen's appearance.

The house was standard for a moderately wealthy
family, but looking at Helen's clothes, I never would have
guessed her to live in such a modest place. Her wrists,
fingers, and neck were all adorned with jewelry. Gold and
diamonds and gems made her glitter like a living,
breathing treasure chest. It was an overwhelming amount
of finery for an ordinary afternoon.

Her dress, too, looked better suited for a night at the
opera than an afternoon lunch with an old acquaintance.

It was a rich maroon color with a plunging neckline and fine silver embroidery across the entire bodice. Small beads had been sewn into the skirt, and they tinkled together each time she moved.

"When did you arrive?" she asked.

"Just yesterday."

Her eyes went wide, and her smile broadened. "And you have come to see me so soon? I feel honored."

"Catherine put your name at the top of the list of people I would need to speak with, so you can thank her for the honor."

"That is so lovely to know she thinks of me so fondly. Now, however, I feel even more pressure to ensure you have a good time. I'd hate to be a disappointment."

"You do not need to entertain me," I assured her. "I am here to get to know some of Catherine's friends and find out more about the city. As much as I love my Aunt Sarah, I do not want to spend my entire time in America inside her house."

Helen leaned forward, her voice low. "What a house to spend time in, though. I could hardly believe the size of it when I visited Catherine while she lived there. It is so fine."

"It is lovely," I admitted. "Definitely better than any hotel I could ever hope to find."

"I'd say so!"

The conversation fell into its first lull, a heavy silence settling over us as we searched for topics of conversation. I wanted to ask Helen more about herself, but wasn't sure what I should already know. I didn't want to admit to her that I hardly remembered her at all.

Helen laughed softly. "I'm sorry, Alice. I feel I should

admit something. Even though I was close friends with Catherine while she lived here, I scarcely remember a thing about you aside from your appearance. And even that has changed considerably since you were last in New York."

I laughed with relief. "There is no need to apologize because I am in the same situation. I'm afraid I was awfully concerned with myself when I was fifteen, so I didn't pay much mind to anyone else."

"Good, then it is agreed," Helen said. "We can start over as new friends."

She asked me what I'd been doing in the years since I'd last been in New York, and excluding every venture I'd participated in that ended in solving a murder, my social calendar seemed pathetic. Especially in comparison to Helen's.

She seemed to be invited to every party and social gathering in the city. She knew celebrities of the stage and screen intimately and referred to them by nicknames and first names as though it was nothing.

"You have to meet the rest of my friends. You would fit in wonderfully." Helen didn't know me well enough to have any basis for this claim, but she was excited, and I was pleased that she liked me enough to think of introducing me around. "There is a party tonight, actually. I know it is last minute, but if you don't have any other plans, you should come with me."

I wasn't sure I wanted to throw myself straight into Helen's social scene, but I also didn't enjoy the thought of going back to Aunt Sarah's and spending another evening trying to dodge Rose's meddling.

"That should work fine. I'll need to go home and change, of course."

"Obviously," Helen said with a laugh. "It will be a wild affair. Wear whatever you have that shines the brightest."

I couldn't imagine Helen having anything in her closet that shone brighter than what she currently had on. I knew for a fact I didn't have anything that could compete. But I would try.

Just then, the door to the sitting room opened, and a young man walked in holding a letter. He had the same brown hair and full lips as Helen, but he sported a mustache and wide-set cheekbones. I recognized him instantly as Helen's younger brother, Henry.

"A letter arrived for you, Helen. Should I open it?" he asked, his voice bored and flat.

Helen smiled at me in apology and then spoke to her brother through clenched teeth. "I have a guest, Henry."

Henry turned towards me, and instantly, his features changed. His mouth turned up in a smile, and his eyes brightened. There was something charming, yet artificial about it. I lifted my hand in a wave.

"Alice Beckingham," Helen said by way of introduction. "You two met at—"

"Mrs. Fisher's home," he finished. "I recall. I had no idea you were back in town."

"And my aunt told me she thought you were away at school," I said.

Henry's smile faltered for a second—just long enough for me to worry I'd said something wrong—and then his smile was back in full force. "Well, what a lovely surprise for us both, then. Or, at least for me."

"For me, as well," I assured him.

Helen stood up and extended a hand. "My letter?"

"It's from Alexander," Henry said, dangling it in the air between two fingers. "Should I read it?"

"No," Helen said quickly, rushing forward to grab it. Henry taunted his sister with the correspondence for a second before he relinquished it.

Then, he turned to me, his smile mischievous. "Helen does not want her brother to read her love letters."

"That is not it at all." A blush had risen high in Helen's cheeks and across her chest. "You know very well Alexander Lockwell is a dear friend. He has done a great deal for you, so you would do well not to start rumors about him."

Henry all but rolled his eyes at his sister's warning and then gave me a small wave as he left. Helen slid her finger under the flap of the envelope. "Alexander Lockwell is actually the host of the party we are going to attend tonight. He is a wonderful man."

The name stuck in my mind, though I couldn't work out why. "That name seems familiar to me. Was he another of Catherine's friends?"

Helen shook her head. "No. Alexander only moved to New York in the last few years. He didn't join our circle until Catherine had already returned to England. You will love him, though. He has been very good to us."

The way she spoke about him with such reverence surprised me. I was on my way to agreeing with Henry that she was in love with the man when Helen flitted her eyes across the letter and then turned her attention back to me as she re-folded the note and clutched it in her hand.

"Mr. Lockwell is a savvy businessman who uses his wealth to help others," she said.

"Like charity?"

Helen nearly winced at the term and then shook her head. "Not exactly. You see, if we are friends, I suppose I can divulge the whole truth to you."

"Divulge whatever you are comfortable with," I said, though I desperately wanted to know anything Helen could tell me. I may have matured from my days of chasing boys, but I still loved being let in on a good secret.

"Our family hit on difficult times recently," Helen said, her voice soft. "Father lost his job, and we were in danger of losing the house. Henry had to leave school because of failure to pay. It was embarrassing."

My parents had lost all of their friends because my brother murdered a man and then was murdered himself in prison. In comparison to their troubles, the Davis' issues seemed more uncomfortable than embarrassing. Still, I did my best to sympathize.

"Well, then Mr. Lockwell came to town. He saw I was in trouble straight away, and he offered to help us out. It is by his kindness we are still in good standing. I owe everything to him."

"He sounds generous," I said, unsure what else to say.

I wondered whether Mr. Lockwell's assistance had procured the jewelry Helen wore or whether that had been left from her previous life. If her family had been in such dire trouble, surely, she would have sold some of it. Though, perhaps Mr. Lockwell had appeared at just the right time so she hadn't yet become that desperate.

"Yes, he's incredibly generous," Helen nodded. "You will see when you meet him tonight."

Soon after, lunch was ready. We dined with Henry, though he was so quiet I could easily forget he was there at all. Helen carried most of the conversation, discussing the wild nature of the parties she attended with her friends, and making me more and more nervous I would not fit in at all.

By the time I left Helen's house with the order to dress in my finest and meet her at the address she'd written down for me, I was half-tempted to feign illness and stay at home with Aunt Sarah. However, when I got home and saw that Rose and Achilles were both still out of the house, I decided to take the opportunity before me—very likely one of few such opportunities—to leave the house without Rose finding a reason or means by which to follow me.

I ate a quick, barely satisfactory, dinner of bread, cheese, and melons and left just as it was growing dark. Aunt Sarah lent me the services of her driver, and I gave the man the address. He didn't say anything to give away how long the trip would be, but three minutes after setting off, the car came to a stop, and we had arrived.

Even from the curb, the party looked every bit as bois-terous as Helen had planned. In fact, if Helen herself hadn't found me on the sidewalk, I may never have found the courage to walk through the gates into Alexander Lockwell's home.

5

T he house was so filled with people that I could hardly appreciate the architecture.

From what I could see between bodies, the house looked new. It had been recently built or entirely remodeled in the last few years. The floors were waxed until they were nearly as reflective as a mirror, and the walls lacked the general nicks and imperfections that naturally occurred over the years.

Music spewed from a gramophone in the sitting room and was loud enough to be heard in every room on the first floor. Tables were set up where men and women gathered around and played cards, drinking and laughing as though they hadn't a care in the world.

I grabbed Helen's arm and pulled her close so she could hear me over the din. "What of prohibition?"

"What of it?" she said with a laugh. "If you want my opinion, Mr. Lockwell has probably paid off the police in this neighborhood to avoid his house tonight. Don't worry, Alice. Drink and be merry."

I imagined what Rose—or Aunt Sarah, for that matter —would do if I came home intoxicated. The mere thought of their disappointment and condescending gazes kept me from reaching for a glass.

Besides, although I had no naïve belief that I would run into the Chess Master on my first night out in the city, I knew I was surrounded by the sons and daughters of the wealthiest people in all of New York. If anyone would know anything about a criminal mastermind, they seemed a good place to start.

Helen was pulling me from what I'd determined was the gambling room into the dancing room when she stopped short and muttered under her breath.

"What is it?" I asked.

Rather than answering, Helen pointed across the room to where her younger brother was dancing with a blonde woman in a slinky silver dress with tassels around the hemline.

"Was he not invited?" I asked.

Helen sighed. "Everyone is invited to Lockwell's parties. My brother, however, was expressly forbidden by me."

Henry and the blonde woman were drawing closer together with every beat of the music, ignoring everyone else around them, and I felt embarrassed even watching them dance. It felt too intimate.

Helen moved like she was going to charge across the room, and I grabbed her elbow, holding her in place. "Perhaps, we should ignore him for now. If you press the issue, he'll only dig his heels in more to stay."

"One short conversation and you know my brother so well," Helen said, narrowing her eyes at me. Then, her shoulders shrugged and she smiled. "You're right. The woman will move on to another man—especially once she realizes Henry has no money. Then, once he is good and dejected, I'll send him home."

The room went silent as the song changed, conversations and laughter becoming clearer. Someone further in the house was shouting for another drink while the women on the makeshift dance floor laughed and shrieked as their partners clutched onto their waists, eager to keep them close for the next dance, as well.

When the music picked up again, I leaned in to whisper in Helen's ear. "What do you mean he has no money? I thought Mr. Lockwell was generous towards your family."

Helen blinked for a moment, confused by my question. Then, she seemed to realize all at once what she'd inadvertently revealed about her brother's finances. "Mr. Lockwell was very generous towards me," she explained. "And I shared that generosity with my parents. Henry, however, has not benefitted much. Despite his many complaints, he has no one to blame but himself."

I wanted to ask more, but Helen seemed reluctant to be more specific, and I didn't want to strain our fledgling friendship. Besides, at that very moment, a long line of dancing people entered the room like a snake and began wrapping around the perimeter, gathering people as they went.

Helen was swept up by a man with a tie wrapped around his forehead, and she grabbed hold of my hand and pulled me along. Everyone in line placed their hands on the waist of the person in front of them and kicked their feet out to one side or the other along with the beat.

It felt absurd and childish, but by the second lap around the room, as the other guests were clapping along and laughing at the scene, I was drawn into the madness of it all.

The dance fizzled to a stop as the song ended, and Helen took me on a full tour of the party, introducing me to the most important people in every room.

"This is Catherine Beckingham's little sister," she said again and again.

"Alice," I would offer, trying to make friends on my own merits rather than my sister's.

"I still cannot believe Catherine is married and has a child," one woman said, hand to her heart. "And living in the countryside. I never would have imagined it. Your sister seemed made for the city."

I'd always thought the same thing. Catherine enjoyed being where people could admire her, where she could see and be seen. Even immediately after Edward murdered her first beau and got himself killed, Catherine maintained her socialite ways. But when we were all in New York together, I could tell it weighed on her.

We'd left London because Mama and Papa didn't want us in such a harsh spotlight, but Catherine grew to dislike any spotlight at all. Perhaps that was why she fell in love with Charles next. He was a shy, quiet, honest man. Catherine needed someone stable after the dust had all settled. Now, she had her family and her quiet life, and I couldn't imagine her anywhere else. I did not say this to Catherine's old friends, however. I had a feeling they never would have understood.

Everyone spoke of Catherine fondly and seemed

moderately interested in meeting me. One man in particular, however, caught my attention.

Helen was telling a young man with thick glasses and oiled back hair that I'd only been in the city one day when I noticed over her shoulder a tall man with pale blonde hair. He stood in the back of the room, almost as though he was trying to hide. Yet, his eyes were focused and unwavering on mine.

"I'm sure you remember Catherine Beckingham," Helen prodded, trying to stoke some kind of memory behind the man's magnified eyes.

He shook his head and frowned. "I'm sorry, I don't. But it is still nice to meet you. Alice, was it?"

Suddenly, the blonde man peeled himself from his position against the wall and stepped into the circle of our group. Both the bespectacled man and Helen gasped at his arrival. But before they could say anything, he lowered his head to me. "Alice Beckingham? Is that the name I heard you assign to your friend, Helen?"

Helen's mouth opened and closed. It was the first time I'd seen her lost for words. Finally, she nodded and stammered out a response. "Yes. Alice."

"Beckingham," the man said again, oddly fixated on my full name.

"That's right," I said with a smile. "Did you know my sister, as well?"

"Not your sister." He said it in an odd way. It was an answer, but it also felt like a clue. Like a ruby hidden beneath a thin layer of dirt. All one needed to do was brush away the surface.

I frowned. "Then perhaps you know my cousin—Rose Beckingham? She is Rose Prideaux now, but—"

"It does not strike me as familiar, I'm sorry," he said, crossing his arms over his chest. His entire posture favored the right side and made him look perfectly at ease with himself and in his surroundings. It made sense considering his impeccable appearance. It would be hard to imagine anyone who looked like him could be made to feel inferior anywhere.

He wore a suit that looked to have been tailored to his exact specifications. It squared off his thin shoulders and gave him a fuller, more imposing appearance than his tall, narrow frame would on its own. His mouth was pink and naturally pouted, making him look moody, though the light shining in his eyes betrayed his enjoyment.

I'd told myself I was not here to find a man, but I had not counted on meeting one quite like this. He radiated confidence and charm, and even though my instincts told me to steer clear, I found myself drawing nearer.

"Then we should become familiar with one another," I said. "What is your name?"

Helen turned sharply to look at me, her mouth parted in surprise. Then, she stepped forward, putting herself almost perfectly between us. "Where are my manners?" she chastised herself. "Alice, this is our host, Mr. Alexander Lockwell."

My hand was already hovering in the air, ready to be grasped. Mr. Lockwell grabbed my fingers, stooped low, and brought my knuckles to his pink mouth.

Warmth radiated from my hand, up my arm, and spread through my center. I would likely be blushing for the next week straight.

"Pleased to make your acquaintance, Miss Becking-ham," he said.

"Alice," I corrected quickly. "You may call me Alice, Mr. Lockwell."

"Alexander," he said with a wink.

The wink was practiced, and I had no doubt he employed it often. Likely, with devastating effects on the females who received it.

"Is there a Mrs. Lockwell I should be introduced to?" I asked, looking around.

Helen opened her mouth to answer, but Alexander beat her to it.

"No. If there was, I doubt I would be allowed to throw such lavish parties," he teased.

Helen giggled, sounding flustered and unsure of herself.

"Oh, I don't know," I said. "Many believe everyone has their perfect match. If you found yours, perhaps she would enjoy being a hostess to your many...friends."

It was hard to imagine any one person could have such a large collection of friends, but I did not know what else to call his guests.

"If you find such a woman, please point her in my direction," he said warmly. "Until then, I will mingle with my *friends* and enjoy myself while I can. Lovely meeting you, Alice."

Alexander Lockwell disappeared almost as quickly as he'd appeared, and the second he was nothing more than a bobbing head in the crowd, Helen squeezed my hand and released what seemed like her first full breath in several minutes.

"Well, there you have it. Alexander Lockwell."

I patted my friend on the back and led her towards the kitchen. "We should find you a drink."

Helen did not argue and allowed me to guide her for the first time all evening.

I THOUGHT PERHAPS Helen had an especially strong reaction to Alexander Lockwell, but he seemed to spark the same kind of awe in everyone at the party. As he mingled amongst the crowd, I overheard more and more whispered conversations of people amazed they actually spoke with him. As though he was some kind of mythical creature rather than a flesh and blood human being. I could not understand it. He'd been charming, certainly, but nothing I hadn't encountered plenty of times before in both London and New York.

Still, there was something charismatic about him. I observed him as he moved about the rooms, and when he spoke, people leaned in. Even in a crowd where I could hardly see my own hand, I had no trouble picking him from the rest. Part of this was his height, but part of it was also that, like the focal point of a painting, it was hard for my eye not to be drawn to him. It was more of an instinct than a conscious thought.

"My brother needs to go," Helen said. Her cheeks were pink with drink, and she stumbled slightly as she nodded to where her brother and the blonde woman from before were still dancing. Henry had a drink in his hand and seemed perfectly at ease in his surroundings. I didn't understand Helen's disapproval.

"He hasn't even spoken to you all night," I said. "Maybe it would be best to just leave it alone and deal with it tomorrow."

"No," Helen said, shaking her head and slamming her drink down on a card table. The players shot annoyed looks at her, but Helen was too focused on her brother to see them. "I'm going to take care of this now."

I wanted to try and dissuade her, but the serious set of her jaw and the narrowed slits of her eyes told me she was a woman determined. The best thing I could do was stay out of the way.

Unfortunately, I rarely did the best thing.

Helen charged across the room, pushing guests out of her way, and I trailed behind her. A helpless kite caught in the wind of her drunken fury.

Henry didn't see his sister coming. He was leaning toward his blonde dance partner, whispering something in her ear, and suddenly, they were wrenched apart.

It happened so quickly I didn't actually see whether Helen had grabbed them both or whether her sudden appearance had startled them and they'd jumped. Either way, they were separated, and Helen stepped between them and pressed a finger to her younger brother's chest.

"You aren't supposed to be here."

I could tell by the harshness of her voice that she was trying to whisper, but the alcohol had affected her ability to modulate her volume. So, everyone in the room had turned to look at her.

"I told you to stay away," she said. "You shouldn't have come."

Henry smiled, clearly embarrassed, and tried to grab his sister's shoulders and steer her out of the room, but she shrugged out of his hold and planted her feet firmly on the floor. She pointed at the door. "Leave."

"Helen," Henry said out of the side of his mouth. "You're making a scene."

She still had the good sense to look around and be slightly ashamed, but it didn't change her opinion on the matter at hand. She pointed again at the door. "Leave, Henry. Get out of here."

"We were just dancing," the blonde woman said.

Helen turned on her, and I saw genuine fury flame up behind her eyes. She sized the woman up, and I had no doubt Helen was going to slap her. So, I stepped forward and separated the two women, turning towards the blonde.

"I think you would be best served if you left this immediate area."

The woman looked at me and then at Helen. She had sweat on her forehead from dancing, but I could see that logic was winning, and she let out a frustrated sigh and walked away.

Now that she was dealt with, I grabbed Helen's arm and pulled her away from her brother. "Come on, Helen. Let's go outside for a moment."

"I don't need to go outside," she said. "He needs to go outside. He shouldn't be here. I told him it wasn't a good idea, but he doesn't listen to me. He thinks he knows best, but he has no idea what my life is like."

Helen was growing inconsolable. Tears were gathering in her eyes, and I had no idea where this was coming from. I'd never been drunk before. I didn't know what was normal behavior, but no one else at the party was weeping and shouting. This seemed like drunken behavior specific to Helen Davis and Helen Davis alone.

Henry's face sagged, and he stepped forward and

wrapped a comforting arm around his sister. "Helen, it's all right."

"It's not," she said, grabbing a handful of his shirt. "You shouldn't be here."

"Neither should you," he whispered back.

Henry led Helen from the room, and I was too stunned to move. Everyone watched the brother-sister duo leave, and I was overwhelmed and tired, and honestly, too afraid to follow Helen outside lest she start yelling again.

As soon as they were out of the room, people began to laugh and joke about the incident, and I needed to get out. I needed a second to gather myself.

Without paying attention where I was going, I pushed through the crowd and walked into the hallway. The kitchen was ahead and to the left, but I could hear more voices coming from that direction. The dining room was behind me and to the right, but the room was thick with cigar smoke and gambling.

I needed quiet and space.

I was halfway up the stairs before I realized what I was doing. Once I did, I was too far to turn back. So, I walked up to the second floor.

Immediately, the noise downstairs became a low rumble rather than a high-pitched roar. It felt like I was half a block away rather than right above it all.

For the first time, I could admire the architecture.

It was elegant, yet understated. The doors were trimmed with intricately carved wood depicting large trees and flowers with woodland animals hanging from the branches and eating the grass. A thick rug ran from the top of the stairs, around a corner, and down a hallway identical to the one on the first floor. Except, unlike the first floor, the doors on this level were all closed.

Immediately, I felt like I was invading Alexander Lockwell's privacy and should leave, but curiosity spurred me on, even as propriety screamed for me to retreat.

I walked past the first few doors and stopped in front of the third on the right.

The room was no different from the others except this door had a lock. Catherine would have teased me for my endless curiosity. For being lured in by the very thing that was supposed to keep me out. Still, even with my sister's laugh echoing in my head, I reached for the knob and turned.

I didn't really expect it to open, but once it did, I couldn't keep myself from pushing the door in and stepping inside. My stomach twisted with nerves, wondering what would happen if I was caught. If Mr. Lockwell came upstairs and found his guest wandering in his private space. The worst, I figured, was that I would be removed immediately and banned from his home in the future, which didn't seem like too great a loss. I hadn't really enjoyed myself much at the party, anyway.

I felt along the wall just inside the door and pushed the button for the lights.

I didn't know what I'd expected to find—perhaps, a bedroom or a bath—but I hadn't expected this.

The room was filled from wall to wall with long rows of...something...covered in tan sheets or drop cloths, almost like what would be used for painting.

Perhaps, this was where he stored the leftover supplies from renovating the home, I thought. However, even that mundane possibility wasn't enough to kill my curiosity. I stepped forward and lifted the cloth.

Underneath the fabric were bundles of wooden picture frames leaning against one another. They were tied together with pieces of rope around the length and width to keep the frames from slipping out during transport.

But transport from where? And why?

I lifted a second sheet and then a third and concluded without counting the frames that there were more here than could ever be hung on the walls of Alexander Lockwell's home. Even if he rotated the art seasonally or monthly, it would take a decade or more before he got through it all.

So, why was it here?

A noise at the party below brought me back to my senses, and I dropped the corner of the sheet I was holding.

There were no footsteps in the hallway or voices nearby, but I had already pressed my luck more than I ought. I turned the light off and shut the door, leaving everything just as I'd found it.

On my way down the stairs, a short man with a thick black mustache saw me and then took a closer look, stopping and frowning in my direction.

"No one is supposed to go upstairs," he said gruffly.

I smiled at him as warmly as I could. "I needed a place to compose myself. I didn't mean to break any rules."

The man softened at my tone and raised a brow, taking a step closer. "That's all right. I promise not to tell on you."

"Who would you tell?" I giggled, genuinely curious.

"Our host, of course."

"Mr. Lockwell?" I asked. "Would he be upset with me? I didn't think he'd mind if I drifted upstairs to escape the crowd for awhile."

The man's brows pulled together slightly, but his lazy smile stayed put. He liked me. I could tell. "It is best not to wander around Mr. Lockwell's home. He is a private man."

A group of people came out of the kitchen and streamed down the hallway, forcing the man closer to me until his chest nearly brushed against mine. I held my breath, making myself as small as possible. As soon as the people were past, I shifted out from between the man and the wall to give myself more space.

"Why? What is he afraid I'd find?" I asked. "Nothing illegal, surely?"

The man's smile faltered, and he cleared his throat, stepping forward and lowering his voice. "Like I said, it is best not to wander. You should come with me. I'll keep you out of trouble."

The glimmer in his eyes told me a different story entirely. I apologized to him and excused myself, walking directly for the front door. The night was crisp, and I cursed myself for leaving my coat inside. I could have turned around and grabbed it, but I didn't want to go back into the crush of people and music and body heat. I felt dizzy and overwhelmed and drunk, despite the fact I hadn't had a single drink all night.

The man hadn't denied that Alexander Lockwell was involved in something illegal, but he also hadn't admitted it.

I shook my head, wrapped my arms around myself, and set off for home. I would ask Helen the next time the opportunity arose. Hopefully, next time I saw her, she would be considerably more sober and more rational.

Regardless, one thing was decided: no more Alexander Lockwell parties for me.

Alexander Lockwell's house was filled with people, but it was much less noisy than it had been previously. Someone had turned the music off, so there was just the chatter of party guests in the air. I was standing next to Helen, enjoying the party considerably more now that I didn't have to shout to be heard, when suddenly, the room went silent.

I spun around, searching for the reason why everyone had gone quiet, only to realize I was entirely alone.

"Helen?" I called. "Henry? Mr. Lockwell?"

I searched the rooms one by one, searching for my friend or anyone, really. Was this some kind of joke?

When I'd searched all the rooms and realized no one else was around, I decided to leave. The hairs on the back of my neck were prickling and an ominous chill had leeched into my skin and bones. I moved to the front door, glancing over my shoulder all the while to be sure I wasn't being followed, but when I finally pulled it open, I was met with stairs.

There was no way out. Nowhere to go but up, so I

mounted the steps slowly, calling out to see if anyone would answer.

When I reached the second floor, it looked much like it had the last time I was there, except instead of a series of doors, there was only one. The door. The same door with a lock I had walked through earlier. I turned to go back downstairs, but the hallway and stairs I'd walked down were gone, replaced by a wall. With nowhere else to go, I walked through the door. I expected to find the room full of framed artwork as it was earlier. Instead, however, I walked into the sitting room of my parents' home in London.

There was a large fire in the fireplace, and I saw the back of my father's head, neck bent forward as he read the paper. I was home, and I didn't care how it had happened, I was relieved.

"I had the strangest time in New York, Papa," I told him, walking around his chair, my hand dragging across the velvet collar of his house coat. "I never thought I'd say it, but I'm glad to be home."

I sat down at the chair across from him closest to the fire and held my cold hands up to the flames to warm them.

"How have you and Mama been while I've been away?" I asked.

When my father still didn't respond, I looked over to chastise him for preferring his paper over human company and came to a horrible realization.

The man in the chair wore my father's clothes, but he was not my father. It was my brother, Edward.

Edward's eyes were milky and blank as he stared straight ahead, unblinking. Dead.

I screamed and jumped to my feet, backing away from the horrible sight.

There was blood puddled on the floor around the chair, and I'd walked through it, tracking bloody footprints across the carpet. I wiped my feet, trying to get the blood off of my shoes, but more and more kept coming, as though there was a faucet beneath me. I walked backwards, trying to get away from the bloody scene, and ran into someone.

Before I could turn to see who it was, an arm clamped around my midsection and a hand pressed into my mouth. I tried to fight the hold, but it was like iron around me.

I AWOKE with a choked scream on my lips.

As soon as I realized I was at my aunt's home and safe in bed, I pressed my own hand over my mouth and waited, expecting someone to come and check on me. Thankfully, no one came.

Rose and Achilles had returned to Aunt Sarah's and were awake when I'd come back from the party.

I could see their bedroom light on as I approached the house, so I did my best to sneak silently up the stairs and into my room. I didn't want to be accosted in the hallway by Rose and her questions.

Apparently, they were sleeping soundly enough that my screaming hadn't startled them.

I slid back down in the bed and tried to sleep, but my mind was too busy with the image of Edward's dead eyes and the memory of the mysterious arms around me. Part of me was even disappointed Rose hadn't heard me and come to see if I was all right. Even though I was angry with her, it would be nice to talk to her. She understood what it was like after Edward died. Blood or not, she was my family.

I felt badly about how things had gone after Rose's confession about The Chess Master. Deep down, I knew she'd only warned me away from the case because she cared about my safety—much as Sherborne Sharp did— but I also couldn't forgive the implication that I was incapable of handling myself. That I would rush headlong into danger with no thought for the consequences.

Mama would blame my pride, but I wasn't prideful. Wishing to be treated as an adult was not pride, it was a right. Everyone in my family saw me as a child, and Edward's death only compounded that. They felt I was too young to be told the full details of what happened to him and why, so it could be no surprise to them that now that I was an adult, I wanted answers. Their withholding had made me curious.

The rest of the night was plagued with restless sleep and disjointed nightmares. Sometimes I was in Alexander Lockwell's house, other times I was walking down the streets of my neighborhood in London while being followed by a tall, dark shadow. I thought it might be Sherborne Sharp, but I was always too frightened to check.

By the time the sun began to rise the next morning, I was exhausted, but ready to be awake and away from my subconscious for a time.

UNLIKE THE MORNING before when Rose had spent the entire meal staring at me and making me uncomfortable, today she ignored me entirely. Aunt Sarah was the one to ask how my day with Helen had been, and Achilles tuned in briefly when I mentioned the small argument between Helen and Henry—leaving out the detail of me fleeing the scene, snooping around the host's house, and finding a treasure trove of artwork upstairs.

"There was a fight?" he asked, frowning. "They were drinking? Were you drinking?"

"Calm down, detective," I said, waving my fork and a chunk of melon at him. "I didn't drink anything."

"How did the host have enough alcohol for all of those people?" Achilles asked.

I shrugged. "He is very wealthy. Someone said he paid the police. I didn't ask any questions."

Achilles seemed disgusted by my lack of curiosity and went silent while Aunt Sarah talked about her lunch with her friends. They were planning a march to raise awareness for women's working rights and to lobby support for the passing of the Equal Rights Amendment.

"Unfortunately, they spent most of the afternoon discussing a clever saying to paint on our sashes," Aunt Sarah said, rolling her eyes. "How do they expect to be taken seriously if that is more important to them than the issues at hand?"

"I don't know," I said with a shrug. "A clever saying could be the difference between people paying attention and walking on by."

"Believe me," Aunt Sarah said. "*'Standing Together Women Shall Take Their Lives in Their Own Keeping'* is neither clever nor able to fit on the sash."

Through all of this, Rose stayed quiet, and as soon as the meal was over, she stood and walked into the sun room. It was there I found her alone and reading the paper.

"Hello," I said softly.

Rose didn't seem surprised to see me. She gestured for me to join her and then returned her attention to her paper.

I felt she owed me an apology for our conversation two days earlier, but I also could not ignore the guilt churning in my own stomach. I reached for her and laid my hand on her arm. "I'm sorry, Rose."

She lowered her paper and sighed, her mouth pulling into a sad smile. "I'm sorry, too. I shouldn't have attacked you the way I did."

"It was hardly an attack," I said, remembering my nightmare and the arms that had clamped around me. "You were concerned for my safety."

"I am," she said, reminding me her concerns had not been assuaged at all. "But I also should have been gentler in my approach. You were tired, and I came into your room on your first night in the city and tried to change your mind. I'd heard the rumors that The Chess Master was in New York, and after the letters you'd sent to me and Catherine asking about him, I knew that must be why you'd come. You have to understand, Alice, the months I spent being followed by him were some of the most fearful of my life. He is a powerful man. If the rumors are to be believed, he is powerful enough to defy death itself. I don't want you to put yourself in the same danger I was once in."

"I know."

Rose stared at me, waiting for me to promise her I wouldn't look into the case anymore, waiting for me to tell her I understood her warnings and would heed them. I could have lied to my cousin, but I didn't want to. The truth was that I had come to New York for answers, and I wouldn't leave without them.

I saw realization dawn over her features. Her shoulders fell, and she looked suddenly tired. To avoid having a repeat of the fight we'd had in my room the first night, I changed the subject.

"What news is there today?" I asked, gesturing to the paper.

Rose shook her head slowly, sighing in resignation. "Nothing helpful, unfortunately."

I frowned. "Helpful to what? Are you talking about the reason you and Achilles are here in the city?"

She nodded. "The case is a secret, so Achilles doesn't want to mention it to anyone. Even you."

"Who would I tell?"

"It isn't that we don't trust you," Rose said. "It is that the information could be dangerous. Since we aren't sure who we are looking for, knowing too much could get you into trouble if the suspect discovers we are on the case. Your relation to us could put you in danger."

"It seems I'm in danger no matter what I do," I teased.

Rose did not think it was funny. "Unfortunately, that is true. Your connection to me and Edward and your family's position in the world put you at a higher risk than the average person. You should always be vigilant."

I knew I needed to be careful, but Rose's stance on the matter seemed a bit dramatic. I understood her feelings, though. She had been through more in her life than most people would ever endure. She had been surrounded by death and attacks and blackmail for years, and it was no wonder it had changed her view of the world. While I had seen more than my fair share of murders and crime, I didn't feel at all like I needed to be alert every second.

Still, I nodded in agreement, hoping to put Rose's worries to rest.

"So, you are looking for someone?" I prodded, hoping Rose would be convinced to reveal something of their case to me.

"Someone." She nodded. "Or a group of someones. We aren't sure yet how far-spread the situation is."

"And it has to do with the museum," I said, mostly to myself, remembering Achilles' comment the morning before that they had a meeting at the museum.

Rose's eyes went wide, confirming the truth of my statement even though she didn't speak to it.

"A thief?" I asked.

Again, Rose stayed silent, but her lips were pressed together so tightly they were white, and her jaw was set.

Thankfully, she was so worried about the information she'd revealed to me that she wasn't paying as close of attention to me as normal. If she had been, she might have seen the paling of my own face. She might have noticed the way my knuckles went white as I clenched my fists tightly to keep myself from leaping to my feet.

The artwork in Alexander Lockwell's home. Row after row of paintings—more art than any one person could ever display—covered with sheets and bound together with rope, ready for transport.

It seemed impossible to think that I could have stumbled onto something like that accidentally. It was so shocking that I tried to talk myself out of it.

If Alexander really was an art thief, would he have

left the door to the room containing his spoils unlocked? Even more, would he have thrown a party in the house while it was filled with famous artworks worth more money than most people could imagine?

If he was a thief, he was a stupid one.

Or was he?

Everyone at the party was in awe of Alexander Lockwell. They treated him like a king. And when I'd been spotted walking down the stairs, the man had told me the second floor was off limits. Did Mr. Lockwell's regular guests know the rules? Did they know they were in the presence of a criminal and knew better than to go snooping?

Surely, Helen would have told me before bringing me into such a place. Then again, she'd stuck close to me all night. The only time she'd let me out of her sight was once she'd had too much to drink to be rational. When she'd set her sights on getting her brother out of the house.

He shouldn't be here. I told him it wasn't a good idea, but he doesn't listen to me, she'd said. *He thinks he knows best, but he has no idea what my life is like.*

What was Helen's life like?

I suddenly saw the night with fresh eyes, and I wondered whether I hadn't stumbled head first into a dangerous situation without realizing it. Perhaps, Rose and Sherborne were right to worry about me.

"Sorry," I said suddenly, holding my hands up in surrender. "I won't pry anymore. I know you want to keep your work a secret."

Rose looked at me with narrowed eyes, suspicious. "Good. Thank you."

I picked up a book from the side table and flipped it open as I leaned back in the sofa. I tried to read the words on the page, but my mind was still reeling with questions and theories and possibilities.

I needed to talk with Helen about who exactly Alexander Lockwell was.

Rose was back to reading the paper, and I realized she could be a source of information, too. If I was careful with how much I revealed.

"You said you remember Helen Davis from when you were in New York several years ago?" I asked.

Rose nodded. "Just barely. She spent more time with Catherine than with me. I only spoke to her in passing."

"She is a nice woman," I said. "Her friends are a little wild, though. I can't imagine Catherine enjoying their company much."

"If I remember right, she didn't. After what happened with...Edward," Rose said gently, "Catherine was looking for a distraction. No one could blame her for taking up with those kinds of friends. I'm sure they kept her mind off her troubles."

"I'm sure," I said. "The party we attended last night was at Alexander Lockwell's house. Do you remember him?"

Rose's reaction was subtle, but there was a reaction nonetheless.

Her back stiffened, and her fingers twitched where they held the paper, crinkling the edges slightly. Then, just as quickly as it happened, she relaxed to normal and shook her head.

"No, I don't think I remember that name."

Rose wouldn't remember it. Not if Helen was right

about Alexander not coming to the city until a couple years ago.

So, why then, had his name caused her such a stir?

I wanted to press, but if I did, I was afraid Rose would catch my meaning and become suspicious. Instead of asking more questions, I tried in earnest to read the book I'd picked up, which turned out to be quite dull.

Thankfully, Aunt Sarah came in after I'd trudged through a few pages to ask if we would like to join her for some shopping followed by lunch.

"Achilles and I have work to attend to," Rose said. "Perhaps, another day."

Aunt Sarah nodded in understanding and then turned to me. "And you, Alice?"

I'd hoped to make my way to Helen Davis' home again to speak with her in length about Alexander Lockwell, but I also didn't want her to think me overeager. Perhaps, waiting a day before reaching out again would be more prudent.

So, I gladly returned the book to its place on the table and accepted my aunt's invitation.

7

Aunt Sarah's driver didn't need directions to get to wherever we were going. Aunt Sarah and I simply climbed into the backseat and the car began moving a moment later.

As we drove along, my aunt pointed out many of the houses we passed and offered bits of gossip on the inhabitants.

"Oh, oh," Aunt Sarah said excitedly, pointing to a somewhat modest home wedged between two identical ones. "The man who lived there was just released from prison last year. Embezzlement charges."

"How do you know that?" I asked.

"His brother is my butcher," she said simply. "I sometimes go with the cook to pick up our order for the week, and he gives me extra roast beef free of charge. And occasionally, a little gossip."

"About his own brother? He must like you a lot."

"Or really hate his brother," she said. "His brother worked his way up the corporate ladder at a bank and loaned him a lot of money to start his own deli. All was fine until the bank the brother worked for realized he'd been stealing money. Then, suddenly, he was in prison, and Marco was at risk of losing his shop. It all worked out in the end, but Marco isn't too fond of his older brother."

"Do you often go with your staff to run errands?" I asked.

Aunt Sarah shook her head. "Not usually. They often complain I do too much around the house already, so I try to let them do their work undisturbed."

"So, why the butcher?" I pressed. Something about the way Aunt Sarah spoke about Marco seemed significant.

Just as I suspected, her cheeks tinted pink. "I want to know the man who prepares my food."

"Do you go to the bakery? Do you know your milkman's name?"

Aunt Sarah's smile slipped, and she pressed her lips together, reminding me all too well of my mother's stern face. "Leave it alone, Alice. This doesn't concern you."

It was early in the day, and I didn't want to embarrass my aunt, so I dropped the matter. Though, I did wonder whether my aunt wasn't lonely. Certainly, being a widow on her own for most of her adult life had given her a purpose in terms of political activism, but at what cost? She had a large house with no children to fill it, and I had to wonder whether she didn't long for a companion.

The driver dropped us in front of a small shop on a narrow side road. Inside, several women sat in front of dress forms, tailoring suits and dresses and shirts, and none of them looked up as we entered.

Aunt Sarah didn't seem to mind. She waited until one

of the women had tied off her work and looked up before she said anything.

The shop already had her measurements, so she left them with a garment bag of clothes to be hemmed, and then took me with her to a furniture store just around the corner. I'd told her I didn't mind the décor in the bedroom at all, but she refused to let me leave until I'd picked out new lamps, fabric for window curtains and curtains around the four-poster bed, and a rug. It all seemed too much considering how little time I planned to spend in the room—especially if my nightmares continued as they had last night—but I could tell it made Aunt Sarah happy to tune the room to my tastes, so I indulged her.

Just as she told me the first day I arrived, she had a line of credit with most stores in the city, so she told the salesman to add it to her bill, and we left, walking down one street and then another before turning onto 55th.

A French name I couldn't pronounce was painted on a dainty sign hanging above a dark blue wooden door. To the right of the door was a wall of windows, through which I could see people eating at small tables. Candles flickered between them, and everyone seemed hunched towards one another. It all looked very romantic for a midday meal.

"This is the best French food in the whole city," Aunt Sarah said when we walked in. "I keep a running reservation here for that very reason."

The host recognized my aunt immediately, greeted her warmly, and then showed us to a table in the middle of the room underneath a crystal chandelier.

The water had frozen fruit floating in it in place of ice

cubes, and we were served warm bread with thick pats of butter before we even ordered. I opted for the veal cutlet with string beans and boiled potatoes.

"I envy your youth," Aunt Sarah said as she ordered her cold cream soup and a mixed salad. When the waiter left, she rested her head on her fist and groaned. "I want to eat potatoes and chicken for lunch, but if I did that, I'd have to let out all of my clothes."

"You could afford to," I said.

She tipped her head to the side in agreement and then shook her head as if to dispel the negative thought. "Speaking of your youth, how was the party you attended last night?"

"Not nearly as fun as you are imagining," I admitted. "I didn't enjoy myself much. Everyone else seemed to have a good time, though."

"Everyone else is stupid," she said with a dismissive wave. "I trust your opinion over anyone else's."

It shouldn't have really mattered, but Aunt Sarah's words made me sit a bit taller. She liked me, and the feeling was mutual.

"In that case, my opinion is that Alexander Lockwell has surrounded himself with a group of people to worship him, and I didn't enjoy kneeling at his feet." I studied my aunt, seeing how the name affected her.

Rose had flinched at the mention, but Aunt Sarah's eyebrows raised in obvious surprise. "The party was at Alexander Lockwell's home? I didn't realize."

"Do you know him?"

"Of him," she corrected. "I've never met the man, but he has made quite a splash in the social scene the last couple of years. You know how it goes. Any man who waltzes into New York with a cartload of money is bound to be talked about. My only question is where he got it all."

"You don't know what he does for a living?"

She shrugged. "All of my friends are too old to know him personally, so I haven't been privy to that information. If you find out, do let me know. I'd love to be the one to tell the girls."

"Helen told me he is a businessman, but no specifics. I'll ask her when I see her again."

"You plan to see her again?" Aunt Sarah asked.

"I suppose so. I'm not sure how else to spend my time while here." That was true, but the information I hoped to get out of her involving Alexander Lockwell was also a primary interest of mine right now. If he was an art thief, there was a chance I'd been in contact with a major crime organization at the party last night. Could any of them know anything about The Chess Master? Then, I added. "Besides, Helen adores the man. I'm sure she'll be thrilled to be given an excuse to talk about him more."

Aunt Sarah laughed and took a long sip of her water. The frozen fruit had mostly dissolved now, tinting the glass a pale pink.

I looked towards the kitchen to see if our food was on its way—my stomach was beginning to growl in a very unladylike manner—when I saw something much more pressing heading our direction.

Or, rather, someone.

Aunt Sarah said something to me, but her words were lost in the thrumming of my blood in my ears. My heart was racing in my chest, and I could barely eek out the words, "it's him," before the person in question was standing at the edge of our table, smiling down at me.

Alexander Lockwell.

"Alice Beckingham," he said as though we were old friends. "How lovely to see you again so soon."

He gripped his hat in one hand and tucked it behind his back as he tipped his head in respect to the both of us. His blonde hair fell over his forehead, and he pushed it back with deft fingers.

"Mr. Lockwell," I said in greeting and to alert Aunt Sarah to who was standing next to us.

Her eyes went wide for a second, but she recovered gracefully and smiled at the man.

"Sarah Fisher," she said, lifting her hand. "I'm Alice's aunt."

"Charmed." He grinned. "I saw you both come in, but I wanted to give you a chance to order. And in truth, my meal was so delicious I didn't want to leave until I'd eaten every bite."

"What did you have?" Aunt Sarah asked.

"The veal cutlet."

"You young people and your lean figures," Aunt Sarah whispered, mostly to me, though I was certain Alexander could still hear her. "Did you have dessert, as well?"

"I am not that young," Alexander said. "I have to be careful. Dessert is reserved for after dinner only, I'm afraid."

"Good," she said. "It's good for a man to have restraint and a sense of his own humanity."

I was used to Aunt Sarah's odd comments, but I couldn't imagine what Alexander Lockwell thought of her. Especially considering everyone I'd met at his house seemed to think him perfect. I wondered whether he had anyone in his life to remind him he wasn't an actual god.

"Believe me, I understand my own humanity all too well," he said. "Especially the morning after throwing a large party. I don't recover like I used to. How are you feeling today, Alice?"

"That's right," Aunt Sarah said. "You two were together last night."

"I'm feeling fine," I said. "I left a little before the party ended."

The memory of my nightmare returned to me, wandering through the hallways of Alexander's home, my brother's milky eyes. I blinked the image from my mind.

"I noticed you did not say goodbye."

Aunt Sarah turned on me, mock horror on her face. "Alice. I've taught you better than that. You should always bid farewell to your host."

"My apologies," I said to them both.

"Actually," Alexander said. "Keep your apology and make it up to me by being my guest again tomorrow night."

His smooth delivery took me by surprise, and I couldn't figure out if he was always this charming or if he was turning it on especially for me. The former seemed more likely.

"Another party so soon?" Aunt Sarah asked. "Then, you don't give yourself enough credit, Mr. Lockwell. You are recovering well, indeed."

"Perhaps, you're right." He laughed. Then, he turned to me. "So, Alice? Do you accept? And you are welcome to join, as well, Mrs. Fisher."

"Absolutely not," she said, waving her hands in front of her. "It takes you a good night's rest to recover, but I think I would end up in the grave if I strayed from my dinner and early bedtime routine. I had my youth. Now, it is your turn."

"I expected you'd say as much," he said. Then, he turned to me. "So, Alice? Will you join me?"

I couldn't imagine a scenario in which I would refuse someone like Alexander Lockwell anything, least of all a personal invitation to a social gathering at his house. Not to mention, I had more questions than answers about his past and his possible involvement in the case Rose and Achilles were solving.

Deep down, there was a part of me that wanted to solve the art theft case before the detective duo could. It would give me great joy to outmatch them and, at the same time, it could prove to Rose that I was capable of pursuing The Chess Master.

"Of course," I said with a smile. "I would be honored."

"Excellent." Alexander pushed back his blonde hair, smoothing it to his head, and looked out over the restaurant as though scanning for other familiar faces. "It will be much like the previous party. A gathering of friends and colleagues for food and dancing. I look forward to seeing you there."

Mr. Lockwell excused himself with another shallow bow and moved towards the front of the restaurant. The host jumped to attention to hold the door open for him, and he stepped into a black car idling on the curb.

"I thought you didn't enjoy his last party," Aunt Sarah teased, her brow arched high.

"I couldn't very well refuse him," I said. "Besides, how

am I going to find out what he does for a living and tell you so you can tell your friends if I never speak to him again?"

Also, how was I going to discover whether he had anything to do with the art thefts if I didn't go to his house again and find my way upstairs? Attending yet another party was a necessary evil, it seemed.

That quieted Aunt Sarah's teasing and soon after, our food was delivered. Alexander had been right. The veal cutlet was excellent.

8

Dear Alice,

Alexander informed me you would be coming to another party, and I insist you come to my house first to get ready. I know I abandoned you at the last party, but I won't do that again. Besides, you can borrow some of my clothes, and you can help me pin my wild hair back in the same manner you pin yours.

Please? I will beg if necessary.

Your friend,
   Helen

Helen's note came the evening after Aunt Sarah and I saw Alexander Lockwell at the French restaurant, and I didn't send my response immediately. Truthfully, I didn't want to spend more time with Helen than necessary. I wanted to prod her for information, but after her near-fight at the party and her outburst, she felt too dramatic to be someone I considered an actual friend.

Then, I imagined how many secrets girls shared in their bedrooms while readying for parties. Surely, Helen would be more open with me in the privacy of her own home than she would at a crowded party. If I wanted real information about Alexander and what he was doing with a room full of art, I needed to go to Helen's house before the party started.

So, I sent a short response in the affirmative early the next morning and told her I would be at her house after lunch.

Rose and Achilles were out of the house starting early in the morning. They didn't say where they were going, but I skimmed the newspaper after they left and saw a small article on the third page about a postponement of a fine art museum's upcoming exhibition. It had been set to open the following week, but was being pushed back with no estimate of when it would be rescheduled. I read the article twice, searching for information on the theme of the exhibition or why it was being postponed, but the theme was supposed to be a secret and no explanation had been offered.

I hadn't looked closely at any of the artwork in Alexander's upstairs room, but certainly there'd been enough paintings there for an entire exhibition. Could that be why the museum was delaying? Because the shipment had been intercepted and then disappeared?

I knew Rose and Achilles would be at the museum trying to solve the theft. Rose had mentioned the case was supposed to be a secret, which meant the museum hoped to keep the public from knowing they'd lost anything. Since the museum was now being forced to delay the exhibition and inform the public that there was some issue, I knew Rose and Achilles were probably feeling the pressure to wrap up the case sooner rather than later.

I had some time before I needed to be at Helen's, so I could have gone to the museum and told Rose my suspicions about Alexander Lockwell. It would have made their job easier if he was guilty. Part of me even wondered if that wasn't why Rose had flinched at the mention of Alexander's name—because he was high on their list of possible suspects. In the end, though, I wanted to be surer of my theory before I said anything. Making a somewhat baseless accusation was what a child would do, not a mature adult, and I didn't want anyone mistaking me for a child.

After a quiet lunch—Aunt Sarah had a function to attend with her friends—I dressed in a pale blue cotton dress and then packed an additional dress more suitable for a party, and went to Helen's.

I knocked on the door, expecting the maid to answer once again, but when the door opened, I was met with Henry Davis. He crossed his arms and leaned against the door frame, showing no sign of ushering me into his home. His mouth pulled into a half-smile.

"I'm surprised to see you back here," he said. "You didn't seem to enjoy my sister's company at Mr. Lockwell's party the other night."

"Neither did you," I said a bit more defensively than necessary. "Not towards the end of it, at least."

His brow arched in surprise, probably at my

combative tone, and then he shrugged. "I am accustomed to my sister's dramatics. Especially once she has had a few drinks. You seemed horrified by the spectacle, though. I didn't think we'd have the pleasure of seeing you again."

"Then this must be a pleasant surprise for you. So surprising you've forgotten your manners and have kept me waiting on the stoop."

I couldn't believe I'd once been attracted to Henry's brand of pompousness. As a young girl, I must have been too fixated on his outward appearance to see what lay just beneath it. Now, however, I would not be so easily fooled.

Henry let out a sharp, humorless laugh and stepped aside to let me in.

"I take it by the gown on your arm you plan to accompany my sister tonight?" he asked.

"What of you?" I asked, avoiding answering his question. "Are you going to be allowed to attend tonight?"

Rarely was I so argumentative with someone I barely knew, but Henry's tone bespoke the authority he thought he had over me. I wanted to disabuse him of that opinion immediately.

His lips pressed together and he looked towards the stairs before resting a casual elbow on the banister. "No, I have found more legal ways of spending my time, thank you."

My brow furrowed. What illegal activity was he referring to? What did Henry know about Alexander Lockwell and his fortune? "Do you mean the drinking?"

Before Henry could answer, Helen appeared at the top of the stairs. She let out an exasperated sigh at the sight of me. "You were supposed to send her directly upstairs, Henry. Not accost her in the entryway. I'm sorry, Alice."

"It's fine," I said. "If anything, I accosted Henry."

Henry's brow flicked up at my lie.

"Sorry, sister. I am not yet accustomed to following your every command." Henry gave me a deep, mocking bow, spun on his heel, and left. Helen rolled her eyes at her brother's dramatics.

"He is still angry with me about the other night and is taking it out on my guests," she said once we were in her room.

Unlike the rest of the house which was fine, but modest, Helen's room was extravagant. Her closet over-flowed with fabric and gowns to the point of bursting and jewels, necklaces, and rings filled drawers, hung from hooks, and were scattered across every surface in the room. Her bedding and curtains were made from the same purple silk with purple fur around the edges, and a golden rug covered the floor, so thick and luxurious my feet sunk into it with each step.

"Your room is very comfortable," I said, unable to find a more suitable word.

"I just had the curtains and bedding made last month," she said, gazing at the fabric with a pleased smile on her lips. "Henry teases me for thinking I'm royalty, but I don't understand why it is wrong to have nice things if you can afford it. Why should I live beneath my means if unnecessary?"

I nodded in agreement, but part of me wondered whether Helen wasn't living beyond her means. She'd told me only a few days before that Alexander Lockwell's generosity was responsible for saving her family from financial ruin. Did that mean he'd lent them money to keep them going or had he instructed them on how to better invest their fortune?

Questions I wanted to ask filled my mind, but I pushed them down and instead hung my gown from a hook just next to a full-length mirror hung from the wall.

"I'm so excited you are going to go to another party with me," Helen said, sitting down at the chair in front of her vanity and crossing her legs. She had on stockings and black heels with a silk dressing gown, as though she was a famous actress between scenes on a film set. She looked glamorous.

"Honestly, I didn't think I would find myself invited again," I admitted. "But when my aunt and I saw Mr. Lockwell at the restaurant, I couldn't refuse his invitation."

"Did you want to refuse?" Helen asked, her forehead wrinkled in concern.

"No," I lied. "I had fun the other night."

She let out a soft sigh of relief. "I'm glad to hear it. When Alexander told me he'd invited you again, I thought I'd have to beg you to attend with me after the way I abandoned you the other night. I am sorry about that."

I waved away her concern. "Do not worry about me. I found my way home just fine."

"I know you are capable," she said quickly, trying not to offend me. "It is just that we came together, and I should have left with you, as well. My brother just has a way of making me irrational."

I suspected the alcohol also played a part, though I didn't say as much. I sat down on the edge of her bed and let out a small laugh. "Hopefully you don't mind me saying so, but I can understand how he might be frustrating."

Helen rolled her eyes. "I don't mind at all. You have no idea. My entire life has been spent trying to keep him out of trouble. At some point, you'd think he would be grateful, but it is almost as though he wants to remain willfully ignorant of what it takes to keep this family going."

Helen's gaze had focused on the far wall, and I had the distinct impression she was saying something she wouldn't normally want me to hear. My suspicions were proven correct when she sat upright, snapping to sudden attention, and pressed her lips together.

"Unzip your garment bag," she said suddenly, jumping up and walking across the room. "Or, I'll do it if you don't mind? I want to see what you've brought."

"Go ahead," I urged her from the bed.

Helen unzipped the garment bag and freed the chiffon gown I'd brought. It was a pale pink color with a layered skirt. The fabric for the sleeves and bodice was a slightly lighter shade. The wide sleeves would reach my elbows and the fabric of the bodice was gathered in a knot just below where my navel would be. The rest of the skirt was dyed a darker color and would hang to my knees in flutters. A thin lace ribbon added details to the neckline and the waist.

I could only see Helen's profile, but her disapproval was palpable.

"You don't like it?" I asked.

Realizing I was studying her, Helen painted on a

smile and shook her head. "No, it is a lovely gown, Alice. Really. I was just thinking."

"Thinking you have something better I could wear?" I asked, biting back a laugh. "It's fine, Helen. I can handle criticisms about my fashion sense. I spent my life with Catherine as a sister, remember?"

Helen laughed and let her shoulders slouch forward. "I'm sorry. My mother has always told me I wear my feelings on my face. I can't hide them very well. The gown really is lovely, but it will look plain compared to what everyone else will be wearing."

"I didn't pack many formal dresses. I'd planned to go shopping while in the city, and hadn't expected to be attending so many parties so soon after my arrival."

"Well, then we will plan to go shopping very soon," Helen said, winking and walking over to her closet. She threw open the closet doors that were already half-open due to the volume of fabric inside. "But until then, you are more than welcome to my closet. As you see, I have more than enough gowns for the two of us."

"The two of us and many other women in New York," I teased. "You must lead a very busy life to have so many dresses."

She shrugged modestly, but didn't specify exactly what her social calendar looked like, and began pulling dresses from the closet and laying them next to me on the bed.

Helen could have opened her own shop. She had gowns in every cut, style, color, and fabric anyone could imagine. Again, I didn't understand how she could live such a wealthy lifestyle if her family had so recently been in near ruin.

"Helen," I said gently, running my fingers along the tasseled hem of a silver gown. "May I ask how it is you have so many dresses and jewelry? I don't want to presume we are close enough for me to know your secrets, but you did admit that Alexander Lockwell saved your family from financial disaster when your father lost his job, so I think maybe I'm not entirely overstepping my bounds by asking whether these things are from your life before or whether Mr. Lockwell has provided them for you?"

My mother would have been appalled by my bold question, and Catherine would faint if she knew how I'd questioned one of her New York friends so boldly. However, my curiosity could not be contained.

Thankfully, Helen didn't seem offended.

"It is a fair question," she admitted. "I confided in you, so it makes sense you are curious. And please, Alice, I consider us to be friends now. I know we do not know one another well, but I could tell the moment you walked through the door two days ago that you would become a confidant. Perhaps, that is why I told you something I have told few others."

"That your family was in financial trouble?" I asked.

She nodded. "Yes. People knew my father lost his job, but many did not know how few savings we had. My father's vices are his own secret, but suffice it to say, our savings had been spent years ago, and the moment he lost his job, we were destitute. I knew Alexander through friends and knew him to be a very wealthy man, so I went to him out of desperation and asked for help. As soon as I asked, I was embarrassed, but he assured me I had nothing to be embarrassed about and that he would help my family maintain our status."

Helen pulled a gold dress with fluttery chiffon sleeves and lines of beads stitched into the fabric from the high neck to the flowing skirt. It shone like a star, and I was certain Helen was pulling it out for herself when she extended it to me.

"This would look lovely with your hair. There are a few strands of gold in your locks, and this will enhance them," she said, draping the dress across my lap.

I fingered the delicate material. "Thank you, Helen. This dress is gorgeous. I'm honestly afraid I'll ruin it."

"If you do, there are more where it came from," she said with a laugh and a gesture towards her closet. Then, she seemed to remember my original question. "Many of these dresses belonged to me before my father lost his job. Because Alexander assisted us so early in our troubles, there was no need to sell anything right away. We did sell our home shortly after, however. Alexander assured me he would give me enough to maintain the property, but I didn't want to be too far in his debt."

"So, his assistance has not come freely?" I asked.

Helen's expression shuttered, and she smiled broadly. Falsely. "Nothing in life is ever free. Alex has been kind to us, but of course we intend to return his kindness when possible. In fact, if there is anything here you'd like, I'm selling it at a discount."

The singsong lilt in her voice sounded forced, and I wondered how much it truly hurt her to be selling her beautiful things. Because by all accounts, Helen loved beautiful things. I wanted to draw earnest Helen back out and ask her more questions.

"You mentioned earlier that Henry is ignorant of what it takes to keep your family going," I said. "What does it take?"

Helen jumped as though she'd been startled and rushed over towards her desk and began sorting through necklaces she had lying on a felt mat. "A dress like that is beautiful enough on its own, but with the right necklace? Oh, Alice. You could be the talk of the entire party."

I could tell immediately that Helen wouldn't be revealing anything further to me. Not willingly, anyway. She'd said all she felt comfortable saying.

I sighed and laid the gold dress carefully across her silk bedding. "I'm not sure I want to be the talk of the party."

She gasped as though I'd struck her. "Of course, you do. Listen, I know you Londoners often look down your nose at New York, but we have some of the finest men in the world. You should follow in your sister's footsteps and find yourself a man while you are here."

"Catherine met Charles in New York, but he was from England, as well. He was only here to work with the consulate," I reminded her.

Helen dismissed this fact with a wave. "He'd been here long enough to have New York sensibilities, and that is what is important. Believe me. You want to be the talk of the party and the object of every man's attention."

Several years earlier, the thought of being the most beautiful woman in the room would have been intoxicating. Nothing would have pleased me more.

Now, however, I was much more interested in going unnoticed and being able to slip back upstairs and investigate Alexander Lockwell's home. Wearing a gorgeous dress and flashy jewelry didn't align well with my plan.

"I think the dress is already going to outshine me," I said. "Jewelry would only make it worse. Really, I'll keep it simple and wear just the dress. Thank you, though."

Helen sighed and turned around, leaning back against her desk. "Fine. I think you are completely wrong. You are gorgeous enough for a dress twice as lovely, but I have already offended your fashion sense, so I'll stop short of offending your ability to accessorize."

"Thank you," I said with a small tip of my head and a laugh.

"But you should really consider meeting someone, Alice. You are young and beautiful and more than capable of snaring any man you choose. You should use that to your advantage."

"What of you?" I asked, wanting to turn the attention away from myself. "You are all of those things, as well. Are there any men you are interested in? A certain Mr. Lockwell, perhaps?"

Helen's eyes went wide, and she shook her head. "No, believe me. I am not interested in Alexander."

"Are you sure?" I asked. "You seemed rather nervous around him at the party the other night. I would have guessed you were smitten."

"I assure you," Helen said firmly. "He is only a friend. Nothing more. I rely too much on his generosity to jeopardize it with a romantic entanglement."

I shrugged. "Well, either way, you don't need accessories and fancy gowns to earn attention. You should use your own advantages to secure a match. Perhaps, that would keep you from worrying about me."

Helen shook her head. "You and your sister are two of the prettiest women I've ever seen. Far prettier than me."

"You are too kind, but even if your kind words were true, I don't plan to stay here long. What use would there be in falling in love only to board a ship and go home again?"

"You don't have to go home," she said. "New York could be your home. Your aunt lives here, and I remember from when Catherine was living with her that she is very hospitable. She would love to have you, and honestly, so would I. Catherine moving back to England just about broke my heart, so selfishly, I want you to fall in love and stay right here. With me."

I walked across the room and grabbed Helen's hands. "Are you already so fond of me?"

She squeezed my fingers and wrinkled her nose in a smile. "I'm afraid so."

Helen twirled around me and went back to the closet in search of her own dress for the evening, and I sat down in front of her vanity and began sorting through her hair clips and accessories. I found a golden feather clip that perfectly matched my dress and slipped it into my hair just above my right ear.

"You have to wear that," Helen said from behind me. I hadn't realized she'd moved back across the room, and I jumped. She laughed. "Sorry."

"The clip will be our compromise since I refused the necklace."

"Deal," Helen said enthusiastically. Then, she nudged my shoulder until I stood up and she could drop down in the chair. "Now, I've picked out your outfit, so you must do my hair."

9

"Alice did my hair for me this evening," Helen said, looping her arm through mine and pulling me into her conversation. "She is very talented. And beautiful, don't you agree?"

The young man Helen was talking to smiled at me, his eyes twinkling. "Yes. Very lovely."

I barely resisted rolling my eyes. Despite my protestations, Helen had been shopping me around to every fellow at the party.

"Thank you." I gripped Helen's arm so tightly she winced, trying to ensure she wouldn't suddenly whisk away and leave me alone with the man. "Helen dressed me head to toe. Without her, I would have come in a potato sack."

"Nonsense," Helen argued. Then, she looked back over her shoulder. "Oh, I do believe someone is calling for me."

"No, they aren't." I pinched her side, and she yelped. The man narrowed his eyes at us, trying to understand

what was happening, and Helen grinned at him
innocently.

After several more minutes of our antics, the man
excused himself to get another drink, and Helen turned
on me. "He was handsome, Alice. And a banker. I can't
believe you made us both look like fools."

"You made us look like fools," I said, unable to bite
back my laughter. "Stop throwing me at strangers. I am
not here to look for a husband."

"What a shame."

I didn't even need to turn towards the voice to know
who it was. Helen's eyes were wide and slightly
horrified.

"Why is that, Mr. Lockwell?" I asked as I turned.

His blonde hair was slicked over, and he leaned more
heavily on one side, looking as though he was resting
against something, even though he stood in the middle of
the room.

"This is a good group of men," he said. "Or, at least, I
think so. They are my friends, after all."

"A clear bias."

"Perhaps," he agreed with a smile and a shrug. Then,
he leaned in close enough I could smell the alcohol on
his breath. "Between you and me, Mr. Roberts would not
be my first choice."

"Is he the one I was speaking with?" I asked.

I could feel Helen standing behind me still, but she'd
gone uncharacteristically silent. If her silence wasn't
because she liked Mr. Lockwell and was too nervous
around him to speak, then I didn't understand what
would cause it. She'd been comfortable enough to
approach him at the beginning to assist her family finan-

cially, but now she struggled to talk to him at a party? It didn't make sense to me.

Alexander nodded. "He is a pleasant fellow. Again, everyone here is a friend of mine. But if you are in search of a husband, there are others I'd suggest first."

"But you don't even know my preferences in a partner," I said.

"Please, enlighten me."

"Well, I'd like a man who is educated but not pompous, wealthy but not conceited, and has a deep love for the arts." I studied his face as I spoke, wondering how my words would strike him.

He blinked several times, and then tipped his head back and laughed.

"Do you find my taste in men funny?"

"Yes," he admitted. "Mostly because the man you've described does not exist."

"Not even yourself?" I asked. I was trying to get information from Mr. Lockwell, but I also had to admit to myself that I was being pulled in by his charms. Despite the fact that he might be responsible for a large-scale art theft, talking to him was the most enjoyable conversation I'd had all night.

"Not even myself," he admitted. "I'm pompous, conceited, and I hate art."

I wanted to remind him of the room upstairs. Of all of the paintings I'd seen, but good sense ruled the day, and I kept my mouth shut.

He opened his as if to say something else, but before he could, I grabbed Helen's hand and pulled her up to stand next to me. "If you'll excuse us, we were just about to go dance."

Helen seemed horrified that I'd ended a conversation with him early, but she would have been more horrified if we'd kept talking. I had a feeling I would have said something I'd later regret.

THROUGHOUT THE REST of the party, Helen introduced me to more of Alexander Lockwell's friends, despite my protestations. And like he'd said, Alexander kept a very impressive group around him. They all came from good families and had many connections in society they were not ashamed to bring up unprompted and often.

However, rather than encouraging these conversations, Alexander seemed insistent upon interrupting them. Time and time again, the gentlemen Helen introduced me to were suddenly flagged down by our host. More curiously, each one excused themselves for what they referred to as "business." I tried to ask Helen what that could mean, but she shrugged and wouldn't even hazard a guess.

When Mr. Lockwell pulled the fifth man away—the first one I'd had even the vaguest interest in due to his knowledge of local crime—I gave up conversing, left Helen with a dark-haired man on the dance floor, and made my way to the refreshment table. Once again, Mr. Lockwell had procured libations for the entire party with no concern at all about the legality, and I grabbed a flute of champagne from the collection of them near one end.

"Amazing he can pull these off, don't you think?"

I turned and saw a man who stood at just my height with short red hair and ruddy cheeks. His eyes were the only feature about him that didn't look as though the painter had muddied the colors. They were a shocking green that had me blinking in surprise.

The stranger must have mistaken my expression for confusion because he clarified. "The party, I mean. It's amazing Mr. Lockwell can pull these parties off at such frequency."

"Oh, yes," I said. "Well, actually, this is only my second time in attendance. Does he host these often?"

"A few times a month," he explained. "Once a week at least."

"He must be even wealthier than I thought. Do you know him well?"

I was tired of talking with men, but something about this particular one struck me as familiar. Familial, almost. He looked nothing like my own brother had, but he smiled warmly and kept a safe, comfortable distance that made me want to hug him and force him to escort me around for the rest of the night.

He nodded in answer to my question. "I've known Alexander since his arrival in New York."

"He came from London, correct?"

He tightened his mouth and nodded, looking as though he didn't really want to answer.

"I'm sorry," I said, waving a hand above my head as though to clear a mental fog. Then, I extended it to him. "Alice Beckingham."

"Walter Miller," he said, his affable smile back in place. "Lovely to meet you, Miss Beckingham."

We smiled at each other in greeting, and then I once again broached the subject of Alexander's wealth. "My aunt told me she believed Mr. Lockwell made his money in art dealing."

Walter's expression remained calm, but his green eyes seemed to turn an even more shocking shade. "And who is your aunt?"

"You wouldn't know her," I said quickly, lying. "She doesn't leave the house often, but manages to keep herself well-informed. She is a professional gossip."

Aunt Sarah would hate to be described that way, but I didn't want to get her into trouble with her own community simply to satisfy my curiosity.

"Not too professional, unfortunately," Walter said. "Mr. Lockwell doesn't deal in art at all. His father was wealthy and died when Alexander was young, leaving him a fortune. He has done his best to be a good steward of the wealth and has invested it well."

"I'll inform my aunt of her mistake at once," I said with a smile.

Walter's response had been quick and sufficient, but something about the delivery felt panicked. Like someone snuffing out a flame while proclaiming the wood too damp for a fire.

Before I could try and discover anything else from Mr. Miller, his head snapped to the right like he'd heard a sound my ears were incapable of, and one of the insufferable men I'd spoken to earlier in the evening was waving at him from a doorway. Walter offered the man a small, almost unnoticeable nod, and then turned to me.

"It was wonderful to meet you, Miss Beckingham, but I have some business to attend to. Hopefully I will see you later."

I assured him he would, and then held my position at the table until Walter rounded the corner of the doorframe. As soon as he did, I ran to it and watched him walk down the hallway and up the stairs to the second floor, trailing behind the man who had waved him over. Sticking out of either end of the man's clenched fist was what looked to be a key.

I KEPT out of Helen's sight and waited, watching as each of the men I'd spoken with over the course of the last few hours reappeared at the party. It took half an hour, perhaps a little longer, but when I once again saw Walter Miller holding a drink and chatting with someone, his affable smile back on his face, I moved slowly out of the room and towards the stairs.

Going back upstairs was a risk, but I knew Alexander better this time. I could laugh it off as a simple mistake, explaining that I'd seen Walter come up the stairs and thought there was a quieter party happening upstairs. I could claim ignorance and escape without too much suspicion...I hoped.

Thankfully, no excuses were immediately necessary. Just as it had been the first time I'd mounted the stairs, the second floor hallway was empty and dark. The cracks under the doors I passed were dark and no voices slipped into the hallway. I seemed to be alone.

The man who had gone with Walter upstairs had been holding a key, which gave me little hope of finding the room I'd opened before unlocked. As far as I could tell then and now, that room was the only one with a lock, so the key must be for that door. And if the man had the key, he must have locked it behind him. Likely, I was invading Mr. Lockwell's privacy for nothing. The futility of it all made me want to go back downstairs before I could be caught. However, curiosity won out.

I stopped in front of the door and listened, waiting. I didn't detect any movement or sound, but it could have been because my heart was hammering in my chest.

What did I think I was finding here? Rose and Achilles were investigating an art theft and had been for weeks. Did I really think I'd stumbled upon the culprits accidentally? The chances of that were slim, and if Rose knew what I was doing, she'd chastise me for getting carried away. She, like everyone else in my life so far, would tell me I'd allowed my imagination to run rampant.

Would I really risk offending important people on nothing more than a whim?

I answered my own question when I reached for the doorknob and turned.

I expected to be met with the hard clunk of the tumblers within the door doing their job, keeping me out. Instead, the handle turned and the door fell open.

When the door was open an inch, I waited, wondering if there were people still inside. If I'd miscounted and all of the men who had left on "business" had not returned. The room remained silent, however. And dark. So, I pushed the door open.

The small amount of light from the hallway illuminated a few feet in front of the door. It wasn't much, but it was enough for me to realize that the paintings that had been there only two days ago were now gone.

I spun for the light switch and blinked against the sudden brightness. When my eyes finally adjusted, I gasped.

The room was entirely empty. Not a single picture frame remained.

As if they might have turned invisible, I stumbled forward into the room and walked the length of it, trying to remind myself the artwork had been here. I'd seen it. Just two nights prior.

The whim turned to certainty in my mind. If not certainty of guilt, then at least certainty that something nefarious was happening within the walls of Alexander Lockwell's wealthy estate.

The way his friends worshipped him seemed more akin to an employee hoping to impress their employer than actual friendship, and Alexander spoke openly and in a friendly manner, but he was withholding. Every conversation with him felt like reaching for a pudding only to have it yanked out of my grasp at the last second. He knew more than he was telling, and I had a feeling everyone else at the party did, too. And I did not enjoy being left out.

As I turned to leave the room, I noticed something glint in the back of the door. I looked and found the key. The door could be locked from the inside and the outside, and someone had left the key stashed in the inside.

Before I could contemplate what it meant, I grabbed the key and slipped it into a shallow pocket of my dress. In the sitting room, I fanned my face. The room was warm from dancing and so many bodies, and I moved to the corner and opened a window behind a chair just an inch. Then, I sought out Helen.

She was still dancing, her eyes glassy with a few too

many drinks. But when I tapped her on the shoulder, she focused on me immediately.

Good, she was not too inebriated to understand me.

"Where have you been, Alice?" she asked. "I've been looking for you."

I grabbed her arm and pulled her away from the group she'd been dancing with, a chorus of frustrated men calling after us.

"What is it?" she asked when we'd reached the hallway.

Most everyone had gathered in the kitchen or the sitting room, so we were alone and drowned out by the music playing from the gramophone.

"What does Alexander Lockwell do for money?" I asked, my voice low but stern. I did not smile or attempt to hide my question behind simple curiosity. It was pointed, and Helen flinched from the force of it.

As quickly as possible, she arranged her features into a lazy smile and waved my question away. "Alice, we should be dancing. Have you had a drink? You should—"

"What does he do?" I repeated, grabbing her hand from the air and squeezing it tightly in my own.

Helen bit her lip and shook her head. Long earrings dangled from her ears and hit her cheeks. She reached up to smooth a hair away from her damp forehead, and I could see her fingers trembling.

"What are you involved in?" I had nothing more than my instinct to go on, but it had served me well to this point. Helen was nervous around Alexander, but devoted to him entirely. She relied on him for money, but was afraid of him. Why? "Is he a criminal?"

"Not here." Helen's voice was a snap, quick and effective. "Go home, Alice."

How many times had I been sent away because someone believed me incapable? How many times had I not been included because my ears were not suited for such adult topics? Not again. I would not allow myself to be cast aside.

"I'm your friend, Helen. You told me this afternoon I was a confidante. Why won't you tell me?"

Helen squeezed my hand with both of hers and smiled, though the expression didn't reach her eyes. She followed a man with her gaze as he moved across the hallway from the sitting room to the dining room, and then snapped her attention back to me. "Tomorrow morning. At the park across from my house. I'll meet you there at seven."

I frowned. "Why not now?"

She shook her head. "Tomorrow. Seven."

I couldn't be sure whether Helen was just trying to get rid of me, whether she would show up at the agreed location or not, but there didn't seem to be another choice.

Just when I considered arguing, Alexander Lockwell himself walked out of the dining room with Walter Miller at his side. He grinned at me, his angular face handsome and flushed with drink. "Are you ladies still looking to dance? I know two willing partners who need to distract themselves from drink."

Mr. Lockwell's voice was slurred, but I had the impression it was forced. His eyes seemed too focused for him to actually be drunk.

"Alice isn't feeling well," Helen said quickly. "She is leaving now, but I'll dance."

Mr. Lockwell looked disappointed, but I gave Helen a quick hug and left before anyone could argue. The idea of waiting until seven the next morning for answers plagued me, but there seemed to be no other choice.

I was down the steps and halfway to the road when I heard a male voice calling my name. I turned and saw Alexander Lockwell walking briskly towards me.

My heart clenched in my chest as he neared, and I was torn between the urge to turn and flee into the night and the urge to move closer to hear whatever it was he wanted to say.

I'd been in his house only a moment before, yet this felt more intimate. Without the lights and sounds of the party, I felt vulnerable in a way I hadn't before, even while snooping through the second floor of his house.

Perhaps, that was what he wanted to discuss. Perhaps, Mr. Lockwell knew that I'd been looking through his things and wanted a word with me. Maybe he knew about the key.

I wanted to reach for it and ensure it was still settled in my pocket but that would have been altogether too noticeable, so I clenched my fists at my sides and did my best to put on a pleasant smile.

"Yes?"

He walked with a subtle sway, almost a limp though it spoke more to his style than to any deformity. One shoulder seemed to rise before the other with every step. As he neared me, he extended one arm. It took me several seconds to realize he was handing me my own coat.

"You left this here after the last party," he said. His mouth wasn't tipped up in a smile, but he seemed to have a perpetual smile on his face regardless. Alexander was alight with amusement always, it seemed.

I reached for the coat, but Alexander opened it and gestured for me to turn around so he could slip it over me. Finding no logical reason to refuse his help, I did just that.

"It is too cold to go walking about without a coat on," he said, his voice tickling the back of my ear.

"I can't believe I forgot it twice," I said. "Thank you."

"Are you sure you don't need an escort home? I'd hate for you to lose yourself along the way."

His voice had something of a joke in it, but that didn't keep the hairs on the base of my neck from lifting.

"I'll be fine. It isn't a long walk. Besides, I think the fresh air will do me good."

I spun away from him and began doing the buttons on my coat, grateful for something to do with my hands. I began walking backwards, tipping my head in farewell, but before I could get far, Mr. Lockwell hurried forward again and grabbed my shoulders.

I yelped in surprise as he turned me away from him to face the street. Then, he spoke softly in my ear.

"Eyes ahead of you, dear Alice. It is best to always pay attention to where you are going." His hands left my shoulders, and his voice grew quieter as he moved back towards the house. "Lest you make a wrong move and find yourself lost forever."

10

I returned late enough that everyone in Aunt Sarah's house was already asleep, so I went immediately to my room where I remained, pacing, for several hours.

Lest you make a wrong move and find yourself lost forever.

It was the second time Alexander had mentioned being lost, and it felt important. Yet, no matter how many times I parsed the words, no new meaning came from them.

Had it merely been a speech of concern? A sign of friendship between us? Or a warning?

I liked to think myself a capable adult, but I did not feel capable compared to Alexander. It was obvious to me within moments of meeting him that he was a man who viewed the world as his to do with as he pleased. So, what was it he pleased?

Eventually, I managed to lie still long enough to earn a few hours of sleep, but I was still groggy and disoriented when I woke up to a gray light streaming through my open window.

Had I closed it the night before? I couldn't recall, and honestly, I didn't want to think about what it meant if I hadn't closed it. Did I really think Alexander Lockwell would be sneaking into my room to rearrange my drapes?

I shook my head to dispel the absurd thought and then looked to the clock next to the bed.

Immediately, energy surged through me, sending me from bed.

It was twenty 'til seven, and I was meant to meet Helen at seven exactly. I was going to be late. I scrambled through my closet, pulled on a skirt and blouse, and ran my fingers through the mess of curls on my head. I'd forgotten to remove the gold clip Helen let me borrow before bed, so I pulled it out and laid it on the bedside table so I could press a hat over my mess of hair and rush from the room.

Thankfully, everyone was still in their rooms as I raced down the stairs and out the front door. I did not have time to explain to anyone where I was going, and if Rose had seen me run past without explanation, she certainly would have followed me or had Achilles do it for her. I didn't want anyone following me this morning. Not if Helen was going to tell me what I thought she was going to tell me.

If I was at home in London, I would have asked George for a ride to Helen's. The chauffeur had become a trusted friend and conspirator, driving me where necessary without my parents' knowledge. He knew how to keep a secret. I was not sure the same could be said of Aunt Sarah's driver, so I had no choice but to walk.

Because of the thick fog hanging over the street and the mist that was growing steadily into a drizzle, I had grabbed an umbrella on my way out. It did me little good, however, because a steady wind came from the side, blowing the rain beneath the rim of my little shelter. Still, I lowered my head against the dampness and continued on.

Few people were out, either because of the early hour or the weather, I wasn't sure, but I didn't mind. It meant there were fewer eyes to see me half-jog down the sidewalk in the direction of Helen's home.

Just across from her house was a small park. I saw the break in the metal fence from a block away and angled my path across the street to the sidewalk leading to it. Greenery grew along the fence and the banisters, so between the foliage and the fog, there was no way to see what was going on inside the park until you'd walked through the gate and walked awhile down the path.

Thus, I couldn't see whether Helen was inside waiting for me already or whether she was late.

Part of me wondered whether she would show up at all. It had been her idea to meet this morning, but it had been an offer made under duress. She clearly didn't want me to voice my suspicions while we were still in Alexander Lockwell's home. Perhaps, she had simply chosen a random time and place to keep me quiet and had no intention of meeting with me at all.

If that was the case, I'd march across the street and knock on her family's door regardless of the early hour. I was not going to walk eight blocks in the rain for no reason. Because the drizzle had progressed to a rain at this point. Despite my umbrella, most of my coat was soaked through and hung heavily from my shoulders. I hoped Helen would offer me the use of her family's car to get home.

As soon as I walked through the gate of the park, my head swiveled in each direction, searching for the shape of my new friend. To my right and left, the path disappeared into mist. So, I chose a direction—right—and began to walk, hoping Helen hadn't done the same thing. It would be embarrassing for the fog to lift and for both of us to realize we'd been walking in circles around the path, never meeting.

I could hear dogs barking somewhere in the mist, alerting me to the fact that there were other occupants in the park, and that thought settled some of the nerves that had crept up on me as suddenly as the mist. I expected to be impatient, anxiously awaiting Helen's arrival and the news she would bring, but I never expected to be nervous. Genuinely nervous. Yet, the hand on my umbrella handle shook, and I had to clench my free hand inside of my coat pocket to keep it from trembling.

I felt silly. I'd been in the presence of murderers. Of people capable of the most violent crimes against humanity. Why, then, was I so upset at the prospect of learning a new acquaintance might be involved in an art theft? It was a criminal business, to be sure, but nothing violent or particularly dangerous.

Even while I urged myself to be rational, irrational fear settled on my shoulders like a weight I couldn't shake.

It had something to do with the way Alexander Lockwell made me feel. The sense of delightful danger I felt in his home and in his presence. People feared and revered him in equal measure, and I wasn't sure where I fell on the spectrum. As it stood, I was debating whether to take my hunch to Rose and Achilles for the sake of their investigation, or whether I should allow them to find the information on their own. Hopefully my meeting with Helen would make that position clear.

Just as Helen reentered my mind, I saw a dark shadow through the mist. As I approached, I recognized it as a bench with a figure sitting perfectly in the center.

An umbrella stuck over the person's left shoulder, partially obscuring them from view, but I could still tell it was a woman based on the curls coming from beneath the hat and the narrow slope of her shoulders.

"Helen?" I called, lifting a hand to my brow to keep the moisture at bay.

The person didn't move, but the closer I got, the more I recognized the amber undertones in Helen's brown hair and the layers of necklaces around her neck. It seemed perfectly like Helen to arrive at an early morning clandestine meeting decked in her best jewelry while I couldn't even manage to brush my teeth.

I lowered my head and stepped off the path, navigating the muddy ground to reach the bench. "Sorry I am late. I overslept and didn't expect the rain, so it slowed me down. You should be making better use of your umbrella. Your hair is soaked, Helen."

Strands of it stuck to her neck and large droplets dripped beneath the collar of her dress. Perhaps, like me, she was soaked through enough that the umbrella didn't matter much anymore. But still, I was surprised she would openly sit in the rain.

As I walked around the bench, however, I realized exactly why she had so little concern for her hair.

An angry gash had been carved across Helen Davis' thin neck and blood soaked the necklaces around her neck and the front of her dress and coat.

A startled gasp tore from my throat, and I lifted my hand to my neck as though to protect it from the same fate that had befallen Helen's.

The umbrella in her left hand was wedged tightly against her side, and her cheek rested against the stick, which had given her the appearance of life from behind. I knew now, however, that if I removed the umbrella, Helen's head would fall chin to chest, lifeless.

"Helen?" I said again, though I knew there would be no answer. I stepped forward, hand extended to try and rouse her. My fingers shook with cold and wet and fear as I touched her cheek.

She wasn't yet cold, but normal human warmth had begun to leave her. Her face was pale, her usually pink lips tinged purple and blue.

I checked the bench and the surrounding area for any sign of a weapon, any clue as to what could have been used to make such a devastating wound. Then, I realized that the weapon was gone, and so was Helen's attacker.

I spun around at once, waiting for the culprit to return, separating from the mist like a ghost to take me as well.

For a second, there was nothing, then a shape barreled towards me, and I threw my hands up and shrieked. I realized only a moment later that it was a dog. A large black dog with slicked back fur, shiny from the rain. He grabbed the toy his owner had no doubt thrown for him and made to run back, but before he could, his owner jogged into view.

A young man with an umbrella and cap pulled low over his face made to apologize to me.

"The mist makes it so I can't see a thing," he explained with a shrug and a smile. Then, he noticed my expression and the scene behind me.

"She's dead," I said unnecessarily. "I just...found her. Just now."

The moments next were a blur of activity. The park had felt secluded when I was walking on the trail, but now that I'd found Helen, people began appearing out of the mist in alarming numbers, drawn by the noise of curious onlookers and startled passersby.

The man with the dog alerted a man out for a walk who alerted a groundskeeper who called for the police. Before the police could arrive, however, several more people and their animals gathered around the bench.

"Who did this?" one woman asked.

"Does anyone know the poor girl?"

I wanted to offer up that I did know her, but my voice had been stolen.

Who had done this? Was it a random act of horrific violence or had someone known the intention of our meeting?

Alexander Lockwell seemed like the most likely culprit, but then again, did he? Helen hadn't been able to reveal anything about the nature of their relationship to me, so I couldn't assume it would have been bad. Perhaps, she had been planning to inform me of an individual even higher than Alexander in the chain of command. Someone who was forcing them all to be complicit in his crimes.

Standing amongst the crowd of onlookers, I studied the faces, wondering which, if any, of them could have done this. Would they come for me next?

"She lives across the street from here," one man offered up, stepping forward. "I know her father."

At that, I turned and left. Helen's family would receive the news of her passing soon enough, and I had no interest in speaking to the police. I didn't know anything, and even if I did, I wasn't sure I would want to share just then, anyway. I needed to think. I needed time to consider.

The reality of Helen's murder didn't hit me until I walked through the door of Aunt Sarah's house and found Rose walking down the stairs. She smiled in greeting and said something to me, but I didn't hear it. My heart was hammering in my ears, and just as Rose stepped forward to ask if I was alright, I collapsed on her shoulder in body-wracking sobs.

elen's brother, Henry.

As my hands warmed around a cup of tea and Rose laid a blanket over my damp shoulders, I remembered the animosity between them. Henry had been angry about being left out of Helen's friend group. She did not want her brother at Alexander's parties and had said herself that he had no idea what it cost her to keep their family together.

Could he have killed his sister?

It seemed too gruesome to believe, but family members had done worse things to one another for lesser reasons. Also, he would have had the opportunity. Living directly across the street from the crime and being able to watch his sister leave would have allowed him to follow her, commit the act, and get back home before anyone knew anything. The fog had been so thick that he could have escaped my notice easily.

"You're sure she is dead?" Rose asked, sitting next to me, her hands folded nervously in her lap.

"I could not be more positive," I said. "I saw her with my own eyes."

"The police," Aunt Sarah mumbled, shaking her head. "We should speak with the police. Someone should call—"

"They were arriving as I left. I didn't see a reason to stay behind and speak with them."

"You were the last person to see her alive," Aunt Sarah argued.

Before I could respond, Rose cut in. "No, she was the first person to see her dead. We don't know who last saw her alive. Alice is right. Based on what she has told us, there was no reason for her to speak with the police."

Rose narrowed her eyes in a way that made me feel like she was searching my very thoughts. Clearly, she didn't believe I'd told them everything. Her instincts were second-to-none. There was a great deal I had not told her.

"Achilles and I can speak with the police, however," Rose said, standing up and smoothing her hands down the front of her wool skirt. "He has been gone since early this morning, but when he returns, we can do our best to find out what they know about the crime and see whether Alice has any reason to be worried."

"Worried?" Aunt Sarah's brow furrowed. "About being murdered?"

Rose shrugged. "Helen was Alice's friend, so depending upon the motive, Alice could be in danger."

"I'm not in danger," I said quickly, giving my aunt my best attempt at a smile. "I barely knew Helen."

"Why were you at her house so early in the morning?" Rose was now pacing back and forth between the sofa and the chair where Aunt Sarah sat, her thick-heeled shoes clicking against the floor like a metronome. Gone was my concerned cousin. Now, I was speaking with Rose Prideaux, detective extraordinaire.

"I was at the park across the street," I corrected, which earned me a glare.

"Why were you across the street from her house so early in the morning? A little damp for a walk, isn't it?" Rose pressed.

"Do you think I may have murdered my friend?"

"Of course, not," Rose said quickly, dismissing the idea with a wave. "But you are not answering my questions, and you did not want to talk with the police. Anyone who didn't know you personally would have reason to be suspicious."

"Well, you do know me personally, so you know there is no need."

I wanted to tell Rose why I'd gone to see Helen, but I did not want her to think I was in over my head. I had a suspicion Rose's worries had less to do with Helen and more to do with the company she kept. However, if I pressed her to answer these questions, she would try to send me home on the next ship and ruin any hope I had of finding The Chess Master.

As if reading my thoughts and wishing to confirm them, Rose held out her hands, palms extended to me as though to hold me off in anticipation of my arguments. "Listen, Alice, perhaps it would be best if you went home and allowed Achilles and myself to figure out what is going on first. Then, you could come back and do whatever it is you think you need to do."

"No!" I jumped up, splashing tea over the side of my

cup and sending the blanket around my shoulders to the floor. "Why should I have to leave? Are you seeking to keep me away from criminals? Because I assure you, London is filled with them the same way New York is. I'm not any safer there."

"That does seem rash," Aunt Sarah said. "Alice only arrived a few days ago, and I don't see how this has any connection to her."

Rose's mouth pressed together in frustration, and she studied me, her eyes trying to convey a message to me. I looked away, refusing to see it.

"I do not want you to get involved in anything dangerous," Rose said, speaking plainly.

"It sounds like you think I have reason to be worried. Is there something you aren't telling me?" I asked.

Hurt flashed in Rose's eyes. She was no doubt feeling guilt at the lies she had told me and my family when she'd first met us years ago. I'd long since forgiven her for falsely taking up my deceased cousin's name and had welcomed her into the family, but I also knew that Rose was better at keeping secrets than anyone I knew. The fact that she had stayed silent about The Chess Master being her own brother proved that. It would be foolish to think she was being entirely transparent with me now.

"It is nothing more than worry for your safety," Rose said, sitting down, her shoulders slouching in defeat. "But if you wish to stay, then of course that is your decision. You are an adult now."

I'd spent so many years of my life wishing for my family to view me as an equal, and now that it had happened, the taste was bittersweet.

I set my cup down on the center table and nodded to

Rose. "I will be staying with Aunt Sarah as long as she'll have me."

"You are welcome always," Aunt Sarah said quickly.

I thanked her with a nod. "Now, I am going to go have a warm bath and change my clothes."

HENRY.

His name entered my mind again and again over the course of the morning.

There had been genuine animosity between the two of them when I'd seen them together, but the same could be said for myself and Catherine when we were in a room together. Even now, as adults, we nipped at one another and argued. That didn't lead to violence, though. Certainly not to murder.

Then again, my brother Edward had become a murderer without any instances of violence I could ever recall. Save for the one that ended in a man's death.

A person did not have to commit overtly violent behavior to be worthy of suspicion. Besides, even if Henry proved not to be the murderer—which I hoped would be true—he could have valuable information about Helen and her connections.

So, after picking at my lunch and dodging worried glances from Rose, I donned my coat, grabbed an umbrella, and set off on the same path I'd taken early this morning to Helen's house.

I knew there was a possibility they wouldn't see me. Helen had only been dead six hours. The news was fresh, and they were certainly grieving. Still, I had to try. If only to offer my condolences and lay eyes on Henry.

The weather had shifted in the hours since I'd been outside last. The sun had broken through the clouds and burned off most of the mist, and the only sign that it had rained at all were large water stains on the ground that were slowly evaporating. My umbrella stayed closed and at my side, functioning more as a walking stick than anything else. I felt like Achilles Prideaux, carrying around his cane. Though, my umbrella did not have a hidden knife at the end. I was sure he had no idea I knew about that secret, but I'd uncovered it while playing with his cane several years earlier when he came to visit Rose.

As I approached the Davis' home, I glanced across the street towards the park. The entrance looked the same as ever, but the foliage along the fence kept me from seeing anything beyond that. Just as well. I didn't have any intentions of going back to that park if I could help it. I was sure the site had been scrubbed, but the thought of walking past the bench where my friend had been murdered sent chills down my spine.

The Davis' home, too, looked just as it had when I'd last visited Helen. Anyone passing by would have no idea of the heartbreak happening inside.

I mounted the steps and rapped on the thick wooden door. And I waited.

There was no sound inside, no footsteps or voices. So, I knocked again.

I folded my hands behind my back and rocked from heel to toe and back again, wondering whether I should knock a third time, try the door knob, or leave and come back later.

Just before I could make a decision, the knob turned slowly and the door opened.

Henry stood in the crack of the door, and I inhaled sharply at the sight of him.

His eyes were puffy and bloodshot, and he looked thinner than he had the day before, though I knew that wasn't possible. It would have been easy to assume he was someone else entirely.

The house behind him was dark.

"Henry," I said gently.

Before I could get another word out, Henry threw open the front door and hurled himself at me. I yelped, but then his arms were around me, constricting my ability to breathe, and the sound cut off sharply.

I would have been terrified if it hadn't been for his loud sobbing, which informed me this was not an attack, but a desperate search for comfort. Even if in the arms of a near-stranger.

"I'm so sorry," I said, trying to pat his back, though my arms were pinned to my sides. "I came to see how you are doing."

Henry could not answer that question for several minutes. He continued weeping as he wordlessly invited me into the house and the sitting room.

I'd expected the entire family to be gathered together in one room, comforting one another, but the room was empty except for a teary maid in the corner. It was no wonder Henry needed the comfort.

"Where is everyone?" I asked.

He wiped at his eyes with the cuff of his shirt and shook his head. "My father hasn't left his room since we got the news, and my mother is tending to him. It is what she does when things are difficult. I can't get her to sit down and accept the news."

"Have you even accepted the news?" I asked gently. "It has only been half a day."

His lips quivered, and he looked so like Helen. The male version of his sister. He shook his head. "I suspect not, though I can't seem to stop crying."

"There is no need to, Henry. This is a devastating loss."

His shoulders slumped forward, and he caught his face in his hands. "She was alone in the park in the early morning. I can't remember the last time Helen was awake before mid-morning. She was never a morning person. So, I can't for the life of me fathom why she would be out that early."

I pinched my lips together. My meeting with Helen wasn't a secret, per se. It wasn't anything to be ashamed of. I'd done nothing wrong. Yet, I had no intention of ever revealing why Helen was in the park. Even though I did not feel I was to blame for her death, her family might disagree if they discovered I was the reason she was out that early in the morning. Not to mention, the worry that I would be viewed as a suspect.

"She didn't mention anything to you?" I asked.

"Nothing," he said, grabbing handfuls of his hair as though he wanted to pull it out. "It isn't surprising. Helen told me very little of what went on in her life. She worried for me, and didn't want me getting involved."

"Involved in what?" I asked.

I'd come to the house to interrogate Henry Davis on his involvement, but it was clear to me now that he had nothing to do with his sister's death. If he did, he was a world-class actor. His grief and pain was enough to bring tears to my eyes.

He shrugged. "I wish I had asked. She was always telling me to be careful, but her friends were only ever kind to me."

"You think her friends did this?"

"Clearly not," he said, eyes wide, a hand pressed to his forehead. "Friends don't often kill one another."

"I meant—"

"I know what you meant," he sighed. "I'm sorry. No, I don't think her friends did this, but perhaps they would know more about who did? Helen only told us they were helping her make money. After our father lost his position, we weren't in a situation to ask a lot of questions. I suppose that is my fault. Helen was my older sister, but as the man, I should have been the one putting myself at risk to keep the family afloat."

"Helen wouldn't have allowed that," I said softly, laying a hand on his shoulder. "She cared so much about your safety."

He gave me a sad smile and shook his head. "I should have listened to her. Maybe if I'd paid more attention, I'd know who did this."

Henry didn't have any more information for me, and after several additional long hugs during which he wept openly on my shoulder, I promised him I'd come back to check on him in a day or two and left.

Rose was sitting at the base of the stairs when I came in.

"Where's Aunt Sarah and Achilles?" I asked.

"Aunt Sarah went to the butcher shop and Achilles still hasn't returned from his errands this morning," Rose said, standing up and crossing the entryway.

I hung up my coat and tried to ignore her presence behind me, but I knew she was waiting to talk to me. She'd posted herself in the entryway so she wouldn't miss my return.

"I'm not leaving, Rose," I said on a sigh. "I'm sorry, but—"

"You don't have to leave to be safe," Rose said.

I frowned and turned to her, arms crossed over my chest. "What do you mean?"

She threw her arms out to each side, gesturing to the house. "Stay at Aunt Sarah's. Read, relax, and go to lunch. Be a woman of leisure for once in your life."

"Rather than meet new people?" I asked, eyes narrowed. "Or is there a specific person you are worried about more than others?"

Rose's mouth opened and closed, and she shook her head, but it was too late. I'd seen the hesitation. The spark of panic in her eyes.

"It's Alexander Lockwell, isn't it?"

Rose looked down at the floor and then back at me. "I'm not sure what you mean."

"You know him."

"I promise you I don't," she insisted. "I've never in my life met a man by that name."

She chose her words carefully, and we both knew why. Rose was hiding something from me. I stepped forward and lowered my chin along with my voice. "I know The Chess Master is your brother. I know that things could be complicated for you, but if you know who he is and, more importantly, *where* he is, you are required to—"

"Nothing," she said. "I am not required to do anything, Alice. Especially because I know for a fact my brother is dead. He died that day on the bridge, and I won't hear anything to the contrary. If you feel you can't trust my word, then that is your own problem. I am only doing what I think is best for you, and I have no other motive."

Guilt twisted my stomach, but I couldn't ignore the suspicion that also lurked there. I felt bad for making Rose upset and accusing her of lying, especially given our history, but my instincts told me she was hiding something, and if I'd learned anything over the last year, it was to trust my own impulses.

I walked around her for the stairs, and my foot was on the bottom step when Rose called after me.

"I'm not keeping anything from you," she said, her voice soft and earnest. "He's dead."

I stared at her, noticing all at once the yellow tone in her blonde hair and the full set to her lips. She'd expressed doubt only a few days ago, but now she was certain her brother was dead. I wished I could believe her. I wished it was that simple. But my gut told me something else entirely, and I couldn't ignore it. I shrugged. "Then there is nothing for you to worry about."

She didn't say anything as I walked up the stairs.

12

I could not leave the house again until Rose and Achilles were both gone, which took two days.

Achilles, world-renowned detective, apparently had nothing better to do for an entire afternoon than follow me around my aunt's home and ask questions about what I'd been reading lately—nothing—and whether I'd been to the theater—I hadn't.

"I know Rose told you to do this," I'd say late in the afternoon when my patience was long since gone. Achilles denied it and asked what the latest fashions were regarding furs.

When Achilles grew tired of my company, Rose watched me. She, however, did not even attempt to hide her motivations. There was no conversation or excuse for why she was following me around the house; she simply did it. When I walked into the back garden for some fresh air, Rose came with me. When I strolled out to the front, Rose waited on the porch. I knew if I attempted to leave, she would follow closely behind, watching my every move. So, I contented myself in Aunt Sarah's sitting room or in my own bedroom.

I wrote a letter to Mama and Papa, assuring them I was safe and well. I didn't know for sure, but I expected Rose had written to them to inform them of Helen Davis' passing, and I didn't want them to worry. Then, I wrote a letter to Catherine. She had not remained incredibly close with Helen, but her death would still come as a shock. Aunt Sarah had sent a telegram the same day as the murder, but I wanted to send words of comfort, as well.

Then, when my letters were written, my clothes were folded, and I'd ran my fingers along every spine in Aunt Sarah's extensive library, I sat and waited. I made myself as boring to watch as possible so that Rose would give up the task and leave. It took another fourteen hours, but eventually, she left.

I didn't know whether she left because of work or because she believed I wouldn't actually leave the house, but either way, the moment Rose and Achilles cleared Aunt Sarah's doorway with the promise to return later in the day, I rushed up the stairs, put on a wool walking skirt, cloche hat, and heeled oxfords and rushed for the door.

Again, not trusting Aunt Sarah's driver to keep a secret, I walked back to the last place I'd seen Helen alive. In a car, the drive was only a few minutes, but on foot it took almost fifteen.

The street was quiet with residential homes on either side and cars parked along the curbs. Couples with prams walked down the sidewalks, oblivious to the violence that had occurred in their neighborhood just two mornings prior. Or, if not oblivious, then unconcerned.

I'd expected news of Helen's murder in a public place such as the park to spark more fear in the community, but it seemed to have gone mostly unnoticed. Part of me wondered whether someone in power hadn't attempted to keep the news quiet. It wouldn't reflect well on the local authorities or the community if New York's elite were suddenly worried about being slaughtered on their morning walks.

I stopped at the end of the block on the opposite side of the street, eyes trained on the house at the center of the block.

The curtains were open and birds pecked at leaves and foliage stuck in the gutters along the roof. It looked like any normal house—certainly not a place where crimes were being committed. And yet, that might be exactly what was going on behind the door.

If so, I intended to find out.

I watched Alexander Lockwell's house for the better part of an hour, maintaining my position on the corner, partially obscured by a corner hedge, and waited. If Rose hadn't been so keen to keep a watch on me, I would have been here sooner. I would have come to see what Alexander did in the hours and day immediately following Helen's murder.

Had he taken in a lot of visitors? Did he pay his condolences to her family? Or did he carry on as usual?

I wanted to know the answers to all of those questions, but I would settle for answering only one: how were Helen and Alexander connected?

As the hour mark approached, the front door of

Alexander's home opened. I darted further into the
foliage, just poking my head around the corner far
enough to see the man himself shut and lock the door,
open and close his front gate, and then climb into the
back seat of a waiting car. The car left at once, and after
thirty seconds had passed, I crossed the street and walked
through the gate.

I could have knocked on the front door, spoken with a
maid, and made some excuse about how I'd left my coat
behind at the party, allowing me access to search the
house. The problem was that Alexander had returned my
coat to me after the last party. I'd attempted to leave it
behind, but perhaps he caught on to my plan or had
simply noticed it lying in a bundle behind the sitting
room sofa. Either way, he gave it back to me, and now I
had no reason at all to be at his house.

Luckily, I'd planned for this possibility.

Rather than walk up the front path and knock on the
door, I veered to the right, cutting across the crunchy
grass to walk around the side of the house.

The first-floor windows were low to the ground, so I
ducked down as I walked past them, lest someone inside
notice me. As I approached the back corner of the house,
I prayed no one had noticed the window I'd cracked open
during the party. I'd opened it no more than a few finger
widths. Just wide enough that I'd be able to push it open
from the outside, but not so far that it would chill the
room.

When I saw the small crack in the window, I nearly
cheered. Though, I resisted, as it would have given away
my location.

The curtains were opened, but not fully, allowing me

only a small gap through which to view the room. From what I could see, however, the sitting room was empty. I slipped my fingers into the gap and lifted slowly. The window vibrated against the wood frame, but it was relatively new and well cared for, so it opened with ease. Then, with a final look around the area to be sure no one had seen me, I gripped the window ledge and jumped, throwing my weight up and forward.

My stomach hit the ledge, and a burst of air forced itself from my mouth, but I quickly pressed my lips together to keep quiet.

I hadn't noticed any help in Alexander's home during the two parties, but there was almost no way a man of his status in a house of this size wouldn't have a household staff. They probably made themselves scarce during his parties.

I waited, listening to see if anyone was going to come investigate the noise, and when I was sure I hadn't been heard, I slid my body the rest of the way through the window and then pulled the curtains closed behind me.

Mr. Lockwell's house seemed larger without the crush of bodies dancing and drinking. I could see it as a quiet, reflective space, rather than just a location for wild gatherings. One where he spent evenings alone. It made me feel worse about breaking in.

Before I'd come through the window, it felt no different than breaking into a public event hall. Now, however, I realized this was a man's home. His private residence. And I was invading his private space.

I brushed away the guilt that was clawing at my insides, crouched down, and moved towards the hallway.

I'd opened the window in the sitting room because it

was the room closest to the stairs that would lead upstairs. All I would need to do was dart through the door and up the stairs without being seen. Traversing the long hallway upstairs without being seen was a bridge I would cross once I arrived.

Just before I darted from the room, I felt beneath the collar of my dress for the key I had hung from a chain around my neck. There would be no point going upstairs without it. I was sure the door would be locked now—no doubt with a spare key Mr. Lockwell had—and I'd need it if I wished to get into the room. The metal pressed against my sternum, warm from my own heat. Comforted that I hadn't lost it, I took a deep breath and darted from the relative safety of the room.

The house was newer, so the stairs didn't squeal under my feet and groan with every shift of my weight. I simply kept my steps light, walking on my toes rather than my heels, and in no time at all I was at the top of the stairs looking down at the hallway below.

The second-floor hallway was dimly lit with sconces along the walls, but just as it had been every other time I'd ventured up here, the doors were all closed.

I counted out the doors as I passed until I reached the door with the keyhole slot and stopped just outside of it, reaching into my dress to pull out the key. Just as the key was in my hand, I heard a door knob turn.

My heart clenched and I had to bite down a gasp.

Someone was coming.

Quickly, my mind flitted through the options: run or hide.

Running could work except I didn't know which door in the hallway was being opened, so there was every chance I'd run headlong into the person I wished to avoid. Also, running would not allow me to look once again behind the door and uncover Alexander Lockwell's secrets.

Hiding would require me to unlock the door in front of me silently and with inhuman speed, but it would ensure I achieved what I came to do.

So, I plunged the key into the keyhole and prayed to be more than human.

The metal of the key and the lock clanged together and the tumblers in the locking mechanism seemed as loud as gunshots, but I turned the key and pushed the door open just as a woman's humming became audible. For a second, I worried that the humming was coming from inside the locked room, and I was barging in on the person I wanted to escape from. But the room in front of me was dark, and when I turned to my left, I saw a woman standing with her back to me and an armful of fresh linens folded and poised between her arm and her hip.

Before she could turn around and spot me, I rushed forward into the dark room and pulled the door behind me as quietly as possible.

I only realized as the door was half-closed that I'd left the key in the lock, but there was no time to get it now. My only hope was that the maid would not notice it and suspect that someone was in the room.

I finished closing the door as softly as I could, holding onto the door handle to keep the latch from clicking closed, and waited. The footsteps grew louder along with the humming, and I held my breath, worried that even the faintest disturbance in the air would alert the maid to my presence.

She passed quickly and without hesitation, giving no sign at all that she'd seen or heard me, but I still stayed silent and motionless behind the door for almost a minute just in case. Finally, when my heart rate returned to normal, I opened the door, took the key, and closed the door.

Then, I turned on the light and faced the room.

The paintings were still gone, but this time, I noticed the rest of the room. Beyond having enough empty floor space to house a large number of paintings, the room also held a series of bookshelves against one wall and a desk against the other. I moved towards the desk.

Clearly, this room was where Alexander Lockwell did...something. The room was able to be locked from the inside and outside, indicating that Mr. Lockwell wanted the space to be secure and private whether he was inside or outside of it. So, the obvious question was: what needed to be kept so secret?

The desk was dark, polished wood and tidy. A fountain pen lay in a straight line along the top of the desk with a blank piece of paper just below it, ready for someone to sit and begin writing across it. A wooden tray at the top right of the desk held two letters that had yet to be opened and one envelope that had been opened, though the letter inside was missing.

Not wanting to open the letters and reveal that someone had been snooping, I turned my attention first to the drawers. As soon as I pulled on the top drawer, however, I realized it was locked.

I ground my teeth, frustrated by Alexander's thoroughness, before I remembered the key around my neck. Once again, I pulled it off, fitted it into the lock, and hoped.

The tumblers opened, and the drawer slid free.

I'd expected to find a stack of papers or stationary supplies, but instead, there was one single notebook tucked away in the drawer. It was bound in leather with a long strap wound around it, and my fingers smoothed over the worn leather as I pulled it from the drawer and opened the cover.

I blinked down at the page.

Rather than white, I was staring at black.

An entire page of black ink.

I turned to the next page and it was the same thing. Page after page of black ink.

"What?" I mumbled to myself, flipping through the first fifty pages of the journal.

Why not just tear the pages out and throw them away? Why would Alexander black out his own journal? Especially if that journal was then hidden away in a locked drawer in his locked study? What did he so desperately want to hide that he wouldn't just throw the pages away? And if he wanted to destroy the information, why not burn the pages?

Then, finally, I turned to a page that had writing on it.

The letters were scrawled and scribbled violently across the page like someone was seeking to tear the paper rather than write upon it, but I could make out that it was a ledger of numbers on one side and names on the other.

The top half of the page had been blacked out, line by

line, but the bottom half was still visible. And the first name just below the black was Helen Davis'.

I slid my finger along the page and found the sum associated with Helen: $5,000.

She'd told me herself that Alexander Lockwell had lent her family money in their time of need, and this ledger was proof that the money had not come from the goodness of his heart. He kept records, and I wouldn't be surprised to learn that he made sure to collect on his debts.

I scanned the list of names beneath Helen's and didn't recognize any of the other names until I saw Walter Miller's near the bottom of the page. The sum next to his name was much smaller, but still considerable.

There was so much more I wanted to do. So much more I wanted to see and understand, but the rest of the drawers were empty, and I'd lost track of how long I'd been in the room. I had no way of knowing how long Alexander would be gone or when he'd come back, and if I wanted to escape without being caught, I should go sooner rather than later.

So, reluctantly, I shut and locked the drawer, turned off the lights, and stepped into the hallway once I was sure the coast was clear. After locking the door, I tucked the key back inside my dress. I didn't expect I'd be coming back to Alexander's house anytime soon—I'd risked my neck more than enough already—but I wasn't yet ready to return the item that gave me unfettered access to his private room.

I didn't run into any maids as I walked down the hall, but I could hear the sound of pans and cooking going on in the kitchen when I reached the first-floor hallway. It was nearing lunch time, which meant Alexander would probably be home soon to eat. Not wanting to run into him when he arrived home, I slipped back into the sitting room and went to the back window.

I'd left it open and pulled the curtains closed when I'd entered, but now the window was in the exact opposite position. The window was closed and the curtains were opened.

I hoped a maid had done it without thinking much about why the window was open in the first place. I also hoped whoever found it open again after my exit wouldn't question it much. Because, from my position on the ground outside, when the window was fully open, I couldn't reach high enough to close it again.

Following the same path I'd taken to get to the window, I walked around the corner of the house, found the front walkway, and then followed it out to the sidewalk. Once I was beyond the gates, I walked briskly and didn't turn back to see if anyone was watching. I didn't slow down until I was back at Aunt Sarah's.

13

A unt Sarah was friends with Walter Miller's grandmother and had no trouble at all tracking down his address for me. Just after lunch, I set out to visit him.

I knew nothing of his schedule or responsibilities, so I only hoped I would find him at home, and I was lucky. A maid answered the front door and showed me into the modest, modern living room. A young girl from the kitchen brought out a tray of tea, and after I spent several minutes sipping on hot tea and studying the décor of the room, Walter walked inside.

He didn't look surprised to see me—no doubt a member of his staff had told him who was waiting for him—but he did look curious. His red brows were pulled together, a slight line forming between them.

"Miss Beckingham," he said, folding his hands behind his back as he strode across the room. "What a surprise."

"I should have telephoned first," I said.

He shook his head. "No, not at all. We are friends."

"In that case, call me 'Alice.'"

He smiled, nodded, and sat down on the sofa next to me. He took a cup of tea and dropped a cube of sugar into it. "If you'd come earlier, I would have offered you lunch. As it is—"

"I've already eaten," I said, waving away his offer. "I didn't come here for food."

Walter's eyes narrowed slightly. "Why did you come here?"

There seemed no reason to be subtle. I had only met Walter one time a few nights ago, and now I had shown up at his home, uninvited and without warning. Clearly, I had something important to discuss.

"It's about Helen."

His mouth pressed together in a firm line and the redness in his cheeks intensified to two angry blotches. "Yes. I heard about her...passing."

"Murder," I corrected. "She was murdered."

"The police haven't said exactly what happened yet."

"I saw her."

The words hung between us for a second. Walter studied me, as if trying to gauge the veracity of my claim. "What do you mean?"

"She and I were supposed to meet that morning in the park," I said. "Helen wanted to tell me something. Or, rather, she didn't want to tell me something while at Mr. Lockwell's party. She wanted to meet the next morning to discuss it in private. When I arrived for the meeting, I found her bleeding and still warm on the bench."

"She was still alive?" he asked, eyes going large.

For a split second, I wondered whether this hadn't

been a mistake. I didn't know who had killed Helen. It could have been the man across from me. Perhaps, that was how Alexander Lockwell had asked Walter to repay his debts—commit a murder.

If Walter thought there was any chance Helen had told me who her murderer was, that would be reason enough for him to cut my throat the way he had hers. Subconsciously, my hand lifted to the collar of my jacket, my fingertips brushing across the skin of my neck.

"I don't believe so," I said with a small shake of my head. "Her skin had warmth to it, but she didn't move or make any sign of life. There was no chance of saving her."

Walter's neck was now the same shade of red as his cheeks and hair, and I wondered how a man who showed his emotions so visibly could be involved with a criminal operation.

"I'm sorry you had to see that, Alice," he said. "But do you have any idea what Helen wanted to tell you?"

"An idea," I admitted, taking a sip of my tea and letting the anticipation build. Walter folded his hands in his lap and leaned away from me. His posture feigned disinterest, but his eyes were pinned on me, fascinated. Finally, I spoke again. "I believe it had something to do with her debt to Alexander Lockwell. A sum of $5,000."

"How do you know the amount?" he snapped. Immediately, Walter seemed to regret his eagerness and pressed his lips together.

"I know your amount, too," I said evenly.

His chest lifted and fell dramatically, though his eyes never wavered from mine.

"What I don't know," I said, leaning forward, "is why

you borrowed from Alexander Lockwell in the first place and how you are meant to repay him."

Walter leaned back on the sofa and shook his head. "You have it all wrong. Alexander Lockwell is a friend. He lent me the money when the museum scaled back my hours."

I sat up straighter. "The museum?"

Again, Walter pinched his mouth together. But it was too late, he'd answered my unspoken question: what would Alexander Lockwell want with a blushing, nervous man like Walter Miller?

"Did he approach you?" I asked quietly. "I can understand how it could have been tempting. To offer him information for payments. After all, it wasn't hurting anyone. Not really."

Walter's face was flaming red now, and he couldn't look me in the eyes. "It wasn't like that."

"He is a charming man," I continued. "Anyone could be fooled by him. I nearly was."

"It wasn't like that!" He stood to his feet, hands clenched into fists at his sides, and I jerked away from him, my back hitting the back of the couch.

He took a deep breath and unclenched his hands, smoothing down the front of his suit. "You don't know who you are dealing with, Alice, and I'd like you to leave."

I stood up and rounded the table at the center of the room slowly, stopping a few feet from where Walter stood, breathing heavily. "I understand better than anyone. I saw Helen's body. I saw what happened to her. Walter, it could happen to you, too."

Walter shook his head, but I could see the fear in his eyes. Of course, he'd considered that possibility. No doubt, the thought crossed his mind the minute he heard of Helen's death. *Could I be next?*

"You could be next," I said, answering the question. "Alexander's reach is far, and unless he is stopped, he'll kill again."

"I've been putting money aside," Walter whispered, his voice barely loud enough to hear. I had to lean in to make out the words. "I can escape the city and—"

"He'll find you," I said. "He has helpers everywhere. In cities around the world. Even in prison. That is where he killed my brother."

I didn't know at exactly what point I had reached that realization. But as I spoke the words, I was confident I was right in imagining Lockwell and the international criminal responsible for my brother's death to be one and the same.

Finally, Walter looked over at me. His eyebrows were pulled together again, confusion written on his face. "He killed your brother?"

"He had someone do it for him. I doubt he does very much of his own dirty work, though I suspect you know that first hand."

Walter looked away again and nodded. I laid a hand on his shoulder. "Alexander Lockwell...or whatever his name is...has been doing this for years. He is far more dangerous than either of us know or understand, but he won't ever be stopped unless someone is brave enough to step forward and give the right people the right information.

He turned towards me, eyes assessing me. For a second, I saw myself through his eyes—a young girl, not even twenty, talking about bringing down criminal operations. It was absurd. Unbelievable. I wouldn't trust myself if I was him, either.

"And you're the right person?" he asked, eyebrows raised.

"I know the right people," I admitted. When the time came, I'd bring Rose and Achilles into the picture. When I had definitive proof that Alexander Lockwell was The Chess Master, I'd present it to the both of them and allow them to do their work. Once Rose could no longer deny the similarities between her brother and the recent London transplant, Alexander Lockwell, I would bring it to them both and step back. Until then, I had to be the right person. At least for a while.

Walter bit his lip. As we stood there, silently, waiting, his cheeks paled back to their normal ruddy color. Finally, he ran a hand through his hair, squeezed his eyes shut, and then opened one to peek up at me, almost as if he hoped I would have disappeared. When he realized I was still there, he sighed and nodded.

"Fine. Let me get my coat, and then you will come with me. There is something I want to show you."

WALTER and his driver must have been in the strictest of confidences, because Walter showed no fear of his driver overhearing our conversation or revealing his secrets to anyone.

"Alexander Lockwell approached me shortly after the museum offered me shorter hours," he said. "I'd been there for years and felt I was due a certain level of seniority, but they clearly disagreed. My hours were cut while another man's were extended, and it was made clear to me that I would be the one let go should it become a necessity. So, my loyalty was waning when Mr. Lockwell approached me with his offer."

"What was his offer?" I asked quietly, unable to believe Walter was sharing his story with me so openly. Perhaps, Helen's demise had shown him the true danger he was in. He was trusting me to hear his story and help him, and I did not take his trust lightly.

"To reveal how shipments were delivered to the museum," he said with a shrug. "He wanted times and dates of shipments as well as the name of our shipping partners. I'd met him at several parties around town in the months prior, and his desires seemed almost juvenile. Like a prank, at first. I was feeling angry, and childish or not, I wanted the museum to hurt. So, I shared the information with no real understanding of what Mr. Lockwell had planned. In exchange, he gave me the money necessary to cover the cost of my bills that month. I was coming up short and looking at secondary employment to keep my house. He assured me that wouldn't be necessary, and I thought we were friends. I was a fool."

Walter turned towards the window, watching the buildings pass as we drove through the city. "It began with a single painting missing from a shipment. Alexander didn't inform me of his plans, so I didn't know whether it was his doing or an actual mistake made by the shipping company. Then, several more paintings went missing and there was talk that they had been sold on the black market. Not long after the sales were suspected to have been made, an envelope arrived at my home. It was filled with cash and a note that said, simply,

'Thank you.' From there, our arrangement become more formal. As I earned his trust, Alexander came to me specifically for information about future shipments. He was looking for more than a few pieces here or there. He wanted something large, so..."

"You told him about the exhibition," I finished for him.

He nodded. "I did. I wasn't sure if he had the capabilities to pull it off, but he did. He stored some of the paintings at his own property until we could arrange for a warehouse to hold them. They are being picked up from there this afternoon and will be shipped overseas to be sold there."

"Why not keep them in the city?" I asked. "Isn't shipping them a large cost?"

"Every art lover in the city will recognize these paintings as stolen. It is safer to sell them in overseas markets. So, he has a warehouse and a ship that will transport them with no official records. To my understanding, he has men waiting to unload the shipments and deliver them once they arrive."

I shook my head. "I don't understand, then. It sounds like this is working out well for you. Why are you telling me this?"

"Because I want out," Walter said, turning to me, his eyes wide and fearful. "You saw what happened to Helen, and you said yourself that I could be next. No matter how hard I try, I can't get out of Mr. Lockwell's debt. He loans me more money constantly, and when I try to refuse it, he doubts my loyalty. He wonders if I'm trying to get out. If I tell him I am, he'll let me go, but I'll end up dead within a day."

"And staying isn't an option anymore?"

"I've been fired from the museum," he said, swallowing down his nerves so his throat bobbed. "I'm no longer useful, and I can sense Alexander growing tired of my company. If I don't do something, and fast, I'll be the next to be found murdered on a bench."

"Not if I can help it," I said with as much conviction as I could. The truth of it was, however, that I felt woefully in over my head. If Alexander truly had people waiting overseas to do his bidding, what was I going to do to him? My brother had been killed within the walls of a prison, and I was no safer wandering the streets of any city in the world. Even if, by some miracle, The Chess Master did get locked away, how could I be certain his employees wouldn't remain loyal to him? The only information I had to go on was from Helen and Walter, and both of them seemed eager to be rid of him. I hoped the same could be said of everyone else.

"This is it," Walter said.

I realized then that the car had come to a stop. We were sitting outside of a warehouse near the docks. The air smelled damp and mossy from the river, and the sun was hidden behind thick clouds, giving the sky an oppressive quality.

I stepped out of the car, my heels slipping slightly on the gravel, and looked at Walter over the top of the car. "Why am I here? Is it safe?"

"No one will be here right now," he said. "And I wanted you to see it. The police won't care about anything you say unless you're a witness."

"You want me to take this information to the police?"

"Isn't that your plan?" he asked.

I didn't want to tell Walter that I didn't have a plan. That I wasn't sure what my next step would be. So, instead, I just nodded. I would figure it out later, and hopefully, he wouldn't be disappointed he'd trusted me. Hopefully, I could save his life.

Walter shoved his hands in the pockets of his coat and walked across the narrow street and towards the warehouse. It was just one of many buildings in the industrial area. Driving past, there was nothing about it that stood out any more than any other building, which was probably exactly why Alexander had chosen it for his business.

I should have put it together sooner that Alexander Lockwell and The Chess Master were the same person. A man who had come from London two years ago with a penchant for art theft and a flood of grateful assistants beneath him, eager to serve. But I never would have for a second believed that I could have just happened upon him. If I could do that, it seemed like his own sister would have had a chance encounter with him by now, as well. Yet, Rose insisted just two days ago that The Chess Master was dead. Then too, the possibility hadn't truly entered my mind in earnest until Helen's murder. Seeing her limp body on the bench made me realize that she'd been involved in something beyond a ring of art thieves. This was bigger than that. Walter's tale of international connections and the black market made me even more certain.

Walter kept his head down as we walked across the street and towards the doors. I wanted to ask if he had a key, how many times he'd been here, and how often Alexander Lockwell himself came to this location. I wanted to ask a thousand questions, but I couldn't do anything other than trail along behind him and take it all in.

If I was right and this was the work of The Chess Master, then this would be by far the largest case I'd ever worked on. It would prove to everyone, Rose and Achilles included, that I was to be taken seriously. That my penchant for observing was more than a hobby.

I took a deep breath and shook my head, trying to focus. I was getting ahead of myself. I hadn't solved the case yet.

Walter pulled a key from his coat pocket and unlocked a heavy chain locking a back door shut. I'd been so deep in my thoughts that I hadn't realized we were walking around to the back of the warehouse rather than walking through the front door. But it made sense. Walter wouldn't want to advertise his comings and goings to anyone who may be watching.

He pulled the metal door open and stepped aside to usher me in.

The space was dark and dusty. Light poured in through windows along the ceiling, and the rays illuminated swirls of dust like smoke in the air.

On the floor, wooden crates were stacked in clusters three high and two wide, allowing aisles in between them. By my math, there were at least eighty-four boxes.

I gasped. "This is incredible."

"It's impressive," Walter admitted.

I looked back at him just as he pulled the door shut. When he turned to face me, I suddenly felt cold. A chill moved down my spine, and my shoulders quaked beneath my coat.

"It's cold in here," I said, trying to fill the suddenly tense silence.

Walter shoved his hands deeper into his pockets and stared at the floor, not meeting my eyes, and I realized all at once how foolish this had been. To come to a location with Walter alone. He'd told me about his involvement with Alexander Lockwell's organization. He'd confessed to the crimes, and whether he'd committed them under duress or not, he had committed them. And now, the one person in the world he'd told was alone with him in a warehouse with not a soul around to hear her scream.

"Well, I guess this is all I need to see." I smiled at him, but my mouth quivered at the edges, uncertain. "I should get going before my aunt worries."

"I'm sorry, Alice." His voice came out cracked and dry.

"It's fine. I should be home in time for dinner."

Walter shook his head and finally pulled his hand from his pocket. With it, came a gun.

I blinked at the weapon, realization settling over me like a dense fog. Eventually, it seeped through my clothes and chilled me to the skin.

"Walter." The word was shock and fear and a plea. *Please don't do this.*

"Helen shouldn't have brought you to his party," he said, stepping towards me, the gun leveled at my chest. "She never should have invited you, and if she were still alive, I'd never forgive her for bringing innocent people into this."

"Did you kill her?" Possibilities swirled in the muddied panic of my mind, questions bubbling to the surface faster than I could ask them. "Are you The Chess Master? Why did you do this?"

Walter's forehead wrinkled. "The Chess Master? Who?" He shook his head, waving his free hand as though it didn't matter. "I didn't kill Helen. I wouldn't, but I will kill you if you don't listen to me."

I didn't know if I could trust him. I didn't even know if I could trust myself. Five minutes ago, I thought I was helping Walter. Now, I realized I had walked directly into his trap.

"What do you want?"

"I told you," he said. "I want out."

"It doesn't seem that way," I said, gesturing to his gun.

"Alexander won't let me leave until he knows I am loyal," Walter explained. "Until he knows he can trust me, even if I'm not useful to his operation anymore. So, I'll bring him you. I'll tell him that you knew too much and were going to expose him and wanted to help me get free, but rather than betray him, I brought him the witness."

Towards the end, it seemed like Walter was talking to himself. His eyes were glassy, and he was scanning the space in front of him like he was reading a mental list in his mind, checking off items that needed to be done. Then, he nodded and turned his gaze to me.

"Sit down on the crate and hold out your arms."

I opened my mouth to argue, but he shook his head and waved the gun. "Alexander already had his doubts about you. You don't need to be alive for him to be convinced you were going to go to the police. I can bring him your body just as easily."

A chill ran down my spine at the coldness in his voice, and I sat on the crate. Walter reached into his coat pocket and pulled out a length of rope that he must have stuffed in there when he went upstairs to grab his coat before leaving his house. I felt foolish for not suspecting anything.

For a second, he stood in front of me, trying to decide how to tie me up and still hold on to the gun. I recognized the moment he looked at me, sized me up, and determined that he could handle me without a weapon. If I fought back, he thought he'd win.

I knew differently.

Walter set the gun on the floor and moved towards me with the rope. Just as the rope touched my wrists, I flipped my arm over, grabbed the rope, and pulled as hard as I could. He wasn't expecting me to fight, and he lost his balance, falling forward into the crate.

Using the momentum, I lunged past him and slid to the floor, reaching for the gun. Walter gave a shout in frustration and desperation and tried to turn around and grapple for the gun, but it was too late. It was in my hands now.

His eyes went wide with terror, and his shoulders slouched forward in defeat. "I'm sorry. Please don't kill me."

"Get in the crate." I used the gun to point to the crate behind him.

Pleading and begging for his life all the while, Walter lifted the heavy lid of the wooden crate and climbed inside. There was a sculpture wrapped in packaging materials inside the box, but there was still room for him to fold himself in the corner. As soon as he did, I slid the lid closed and reached for the crate on the stack next to it.

Each crate was full of artwork and the wood itself was

very heavy, but I was able to slide it over the top of Walter's crate, sealing him inside.

"Alice, please," he cried, his voice muffled. "Don't leave me here."

I took note of where the crate was located in the warehouse so I could send help for him later, and then I pocketed the gun and ran.

14

I didn't check to see whether Walter's driver was still waiting in front of the warehouse or not. Clearly, Walter trusted the man, which meant I could not. If he saw me leave the warehouse without Walter, he could alert Alexander that something was wrong.

He could have already left to do that very thing. Maybe that was why Walter wanted to tie me up. To have me ready for when his driver returned to the warehouse with Mr. Lockwell in tow.

I had no idea what Walter's entire plan was, but I knew that I had to make sure Alexander Lockwell didn't get away. Not this time.

I walked through the back alleys of the warehouse district until I reached a busy road and flagged down a passing cab.

After the hour I'd just had, it felt like it should have been obvious to everyone who looked at me what I'd been through, but then I realized that I was physically unscathed. Despite being whisked across the city, nearly kidnapped and bound in a warehouse, and used as a trade for someone's freedom, I was completely unharmed. Not even my clothing was askew. It was a miracle.

No, an accomplishment. I could have obeyed Walter's orders and let him tie my wrists, but I fought. That was something to be proud of. I got myself out of that situation, and I would get myself out of the rest of this mess, too. I was more than capable.

But first, I needed to get to Alexander Lockwell's house.

It would be foolish to go into his house alone. I knew I could not face him on my own and win. But I wanted to make sure that he was at home before I alerted the police. There would be no sense in calling the police, having them swarm his home, and then realize he wasn't home in the first place. All that would do was give his household staff and associates time to warn him that his plan had been foiled, and he would run. I did not want to give Alexander that opportunity.

I wanted to check to see how many bullets were in the gun, but I didn't think the cab driver would appreciate his passenger playing with a weapon in his backseat, so I kept it in the pocket of my coat, my hand pressed against the cool metal the whole time for reassurance.

When the cab driver pulled up along the curb a few blocks from Mr. Lockwell's, I paid him, leaving a handsome tip, and approached the house from the opposite side of the street, wanting plenty of distance between myself and the property lest something was to go wrong.

The list of things I believed could go wrong was long. Endless, really. Someone could have warned The Chess

Master that I was coming for him, and he could escape.
Someone could have warned him I was coming for him,
and he could not care. Someone as connected as
Alexander seemed to be no doubt had connections
within the police force. Maybe he wasn't worried at all
about being caught because he knew it wasn't possible. In
that case, he could discover I knew his true identity and
have me killed.

Scenario after scenario played out in my head all at
the same time, crowding my thoughts until I could think
of nothing but failure.

"No," I said to myself, shaking my head.

A woman pushing a pram with a small pink baby
inside looked up at me warily, and I smiled at her, trying
to silently assure her I was not a lunatic.

No, I thought to myself. *I will succeed. I have to.*

The thought of standing across the street and waiting
for a sighting of Alexander Lockwell was appealing,
mostly because it would allow me to maintain a safe
distance from his home and possible danger. However, it
also required more time than I had. I needed to lay eyes
on Alexander soon before I could alert the police and
Rose to his location. So, I gripped the gun in my pocket
for courage and strode across the street, keeping my head
down.

The gate in front of the house opened smoothly
without so much as a squeak, and I suspected Alexander
kept it well oiled to keep the comings and goings of
himself and his associates as private from his neighbors
as possible. In this case, it worked out for me, as well.

Taking the same path across the yard that I'd taken
only earlier this morning—it felt like it could have been

days ago—I crouched around the corner of the house
and walked to the window at the back corner. I sighed
when I got there. The window and curtains both had
been closed, allowing me no view inside.

I turned and leaned my back against the wall, trying
to think. Trying to remember the layout of the house and
any other vantage points inside.

Using the front of the house was not an option. I did
not want Alexander to see me on his porch or snooping
around his front windows. There was a back door with a
window, but it had a view into the kitchen, which was one
of the last rooms Alexander would likely be seen in.

I dropped my chin to my chest and closed my eyes,
taking a deep breath to clear my head. Then, I opened my
eyes, ready to walk the perimeter of the house and check
through every window. That was when I saw the end of a
stick poking out from under the bush next to me.

It was not a twig or a branch, it was a polished stick. A
long, straight stick with a bit of metal on the tip.

My heart sputtered at the sight, and I blinked, hoping
I was seeing things. I bent down slowly to pick it up, and
more length revealed itself from inside the bush. As I
pulled it free, I saw the curved handle at the top.

It was a cane.

My hand shook as I gripped the top of the cane and
felt the secret release lever right by my index finger. I hit
the lever and a hidden knife slid from the end of the
cane. A single sob forced itself from between my lips.

I was holding Achilles Prideaux's cane.

The cane he took with him everywhere. The cane I'd
never seen him without. And there it was, lying on the
ground next to Alexander Lockwell's home.

Of all the possible things that could have gone wrong to ruin my plan, the possibility that my cousin's husband could have been kidnapped by her murderous brother had never once crossed my mind. But now, it was the worst thing I could possibly think of.

I DROPPED the cane back on the ground and kicked it behind the bush. I couldn't carry it with me. If I did, it would be immediately obvious that I knew what was going on. So, I left it behind as I walked back around the house and mounted the steps to the front porch. I took one deep breath before knocking three times and standing back.

A maid answered the door. She smiled sweetly, innocently, and I wondered whether she knew what was happening inside the house. If so, the house was filled with criminals. Anyone who could carry on cleaning a house and cooking food for someone who routinely kidnapped and murdered people was just as guilty as the person doing the kidnapping and murdering.

Still, I tried to remain smiling and pleasant while these thoughts were tumbling through my head.

"I'm here for Mr. Lockwell," I said.

The maid's eyebrows flicked upwards for only an instant before she shook her head. "I'm sorry, miss. He isn't here."

"Are you certain?" I asked. "He requested I come immediately. It is for business."

Business. The word that had been thrown out time and time again at the party as men had excused themselves from my company to meet with Alexander. It meant something to Alexander, and it clearly meant something to the maid.

Where she had been calm and confident before, she was now shifting nervously from side to side, her hand gripping the edge of the door, unsure of whether she should close it in my face or throw it open.

"I'm happy to wait in the sitting room for him to return," I said.

The maid bit her lip, and she looked so young. No older than twenty. Surely, she couldn't know what was going on in the house. Likely, she only knew enough to know she should be afraid of disappointing Mr. Lockwell, which would explain her indecision.

I leaned forward, whispering. "I think he would be upset if you sent me away."

That seemed to make her decision for her. All at once, the maid opened the door and ushered me inside. She offered to take my coat, but I told her I would keep it.

"I'm still cold from my walk," I said. Though, my attachment to the garment had much more to do with the fact that Walter's gun was in the front pocket.

She showed me to the sitting room and offered me tea while I waited, but I declined.

The maid stood in the doorway between the sitting room and the hallway. She glanced up towards the stairs and then back at me, and I could see her warring with herself. She'd told me Mr. Lockwell wasn't home, but we both knew he was right upstairs. Probably in the room he kept locked. Likely a room the maid was not allowed to disturb him in. But if this was business, should she disturb him now? Her thoughts were written plainly on her face, and I smiled at her, waiting for her to make her decision. Regardless of what she did, I would be going up those stairs at the soonest possible moment.

"Excuse me," she said softly, turning on her heel and taking the stairs two at a time.

I stood as soon as she was out of sight and followed behind her.

My movements were sure and steady, but only because they had to be. Because I had no other option. There wasn't time or room for fear or uncertainty. I'd chosen this path, and now I had to stay the course.

I ignored the shaking in my hand as I slipped it into the coat pocket and gripped the gun.

The maid was knocking on the door when I reached the top of the stairs. Her knuckles rapped on the wood quickly, as though the door was hot to the touch and she didn't wish to get burned.

I hung back, keeping just out of direct view, waiting for the door to open. Waiting until I saw Alexander before I made my next move.

A muffled voice came from behind the door, and the maid flinched.

"It's Miriam," she said softly. I presumed that was her own name. "There is someone here to see you. For business," she added after a brief hesitation. Her hands twisted behind her back, tangling together until I wasn't sure she'd be able to pull them apart.

As soon as the door opened, however, her hands sprung apart and jumped out towards her sides as she took a quick step away from the door.

Whatever she knew about Alexander Lockwell, she knew enough to be terrified.

"Business?" Alexander asked.

"Business," I said, stepping out of the shadows, arms extended with the gun in my hands. Thankfully, it didn't shake.

The maid screamed and cowered against the wall, but Alexander was unshaken. If anything, he looked amused.

"Alice Beckingham," he broke my last name down into syllables, spitting it at me like bullets. "Why am I not surprised?"

"Probably because you've dealt with us Beckinghams before," I said, taking slow, deliberate steps towards him.

His blonde eyebrow arched. He could deny it, but I'd lobbed a ball at him, and Alexander couldn't resist playing.

"Ahh, yes, but the last Beckingham I dealt with was not nearly as clever."

I hated hearing him talk about my brother. Especially since I now knew he was the man who'd had him killed —he was the man who had helped my brother end up in prison in the first place. But I couldn't allow myself to be emotional about any of that yet. Achilles' life depended on me keeping a cool head.

The maid was sobbing against the wall, and Alexander glared at her, frightening her into silence.

"Where's Monsieur Prideaux?" I asked. "I'm here to take him with me."

His mouth broke into a full grin. "Here I thought I'd caught the detective who was after me, but turns out, there were two."

"Three," I corrected. "If you count your sister."

At that, Alexander's eyes narrowed. I knew more than he expected, and I had a feeling The Chess Master did not enjoy being surprised. "Things are growing more interesting by the second."

"They will continue to do so unless you bring Achilles to me, unharmed."

He pouted out his lower lip. "That would ruin my fun."

I lifted the gun, leveling it at his chest. "I could also ruin your fun. Permanently."

Alexander glanced through the open door of his study and then back to me, lifting his chin. "I'm not sure your cousin would appreciate that."

"She'll understand when she discovers I did it to save her husband. I'm sure he means more to her than you do."

If it was possible for The Chess Master to have feelings, that may have hurt them. His lips pressed together in frustration, and he clenched a fist at his side, flexing his fingers. "How did you know Achilles was here?"

"Why did you kill Helen Davis?" I asked, responding to his question with one of my own. I did not owe The Chess Master any answers. I was the one with the weapon, and he was the one who had killed my brother. He would be the one on trial if I had anything to say about it.

He shrugged and had the audacity to look bored. "You were the one going to meet her to gather information about me. Surely you can guess why she needed to die. I can't allow those in my debt to betray me. It doesn't reflect well on my business."

"It had nothing to do with the $5,000 she owed you?"

Alexander studied me for a second and then opened his mouth, looking like he was going to say something, before he closed it again and glanced into his study towards where I knew the desk was positioned. I saw the moment it all registered on his face, and he smiled. "You are better than I expected, Alice. I assumed I had lost the key, but—"

I reached into the collar of my dress with my free hand and pulled out the key that was still on a chain around my neck. Alexander grinned broadly and shook his head. "If things were different, I'd hire you."

"You'd blackmail me, correct?" I asked. "Isn't that how you keep people employed? That's what Walter told me, anyway."

"Walter?" His face darkened. "What did Walter tell you? Where is he?"

"Sleeping in a crate, I presume," I said, trying to master the same bored tone Alexander was capable of. "I don't suppose he is dead, but I'm also not sure how airtight the box was. He could have suffocated by now."

There was a wicked spark of amusement behind Alexander's eyes, and then he shook his head. "Helen's death had nothing to do with the money she owed. I enjoy having people in my debt. It makes them much more willing to assist me when I require it. Unfortunately, Helen's death had everything to do with your curiosity."

Guilt twisted in my stomach, and I fought back the emotions that threatened to rise to the surface.

"You forced me to kill your friend."

The words hit me like a physical blow, and I had to reposition my hand on the gun, forcing myself to stay focused.

"No, *you* killed her. I did not make that decision. I did

not force you to do anything. You killed Helen because it benefitted you." I spoke loudly and clearly, allowing myself to absorb and believe the words, as well. None of this was my fault. No matter what Alexander said, he was the one responsible for Helen's death. Not me.

"Helen made her choices," Alexander said. "Just as Achilles made his. I knew my sister was in the city, but I did not seek her out. I would have left them both alone, but he came to me, and he got what he deserved."

My eyes widened as I understood his words. "What did he get? What did you do?"

He smiled, his mouth twisting into a sinister expression that made my chest constrict. "Nothing...yet."

I sighed, and Alexander chuckled.

He enjoyed making me squirm. People were nothing more than ants to him. Insignificant things he could play with and torture as he wished.

"Achilles?" I shouted, tired of playing this game. The longer I spent inside Alexander's house, the more it felt like I wouldn't find my way out. "Achilles, are you here?"

There was a rustling from inside the room, and Alexander's eyebrows lifted in surprise. "Oh, he is finally waking up. Good. We can get started."

"No, you can't," I said between gritted teeth, taking another step closer. "I'll kill you, Alexander. I mean it. Let him go, or I'll shoot."

"If you're going to shoot me, you may as well call me by my real name," he said. He tipped his head as if in greeting, playing at being a gentleman. "Jimmy Dennet."

"I'll kill you, Jimmy."

The Chess Master took a step away from the door, his eyes narrowed, and for the first time, I realized exactly what this man was capable of. Even knowing what he had done, I had imagined we were still living within polite society. It seemed impossible that he would charge down the hallway and attack me, but that image suddenly flashed in my mind, and I realized how possible it was. More than that, I realized it was likely.

Alexander wouldn't let me leave his house. Not knowing what I knew. He was talking about taking care of Achilles, but Alexander expected me to be right there next to him. He'd end us both without losing a minute of sleep.

"I will," he growled as if reading my thoughts on my face. His expression was dark now, and the maid covered her ears as though trying to protect herself. The way she was trembling told me this was the first time she'd seen overt violence like this. She was terrified.

I only looked at the maid for a second, but it was long enough for a second figure to appear in the doorway behind The Chess Master.

His eye was purple and swollen, so it took me a second to recognize Achilles. By the time I did, he had a chair lifted over his head and was bringing it down.

Alexander saw my attention shift from his, and he threw himself to one side of the hallway, just dodging Achilles' blow.

Achilles shouted in frustration and grabbed for the chair again, but Alexander kicked out at him, a foot landing firmly in the detective's chest. Achilles stumbled back, maintaining his grip on the chair, and swung it clumsily towards Alexander. A chair leg caught Alexander in the side, and he groaned and grabbed at his ribs.

That was when I saw it, his fear.

The Chess Master was afraid.

He ducked below the next swing of the chair and rather than staying to fight, he ran down the hallway directly towards me.

For a second, I froze. Then, I took a breath and pulled the trigger.

The gun clicked, but nothing else happened. There weren't any bullets. It was empty, and The Chess Master was running straight for me.

15

I braced myself for impact, preparing for a fight, but Alexander just shoved me to the side and ran down the stairs.

Achilles tried to give chase, but he tripped over his own feet and fell down, landing hard on one knee and bracing himself on the chair in his hands as though it was his cane.

"Achilles." I dropped the gun and rushed forward, laying my hand on his shoulder. "Are you all right? Are you hurt?"

He shook his head and tried to keep moving, but his eyes were glazed over and unfocused. Whatever burst of energy had allowed him to rush from the room and attack Alexander was fading quickly.

"Stop," I said, pressing him down to the floor. Despite his size advantage over me, it was incredibly easy to force him down. "You need to rest."

"I can't," he growled. "He is getting away."

I had the same urge as Achilles. "I want to chase after

him, too, but what I want more than that is for you to make it back to Rose in one piece. So, sit. Rest."

Unable to fight it anymore, Achilles slouched back against the wall, breathing heavily. The maid was still cowering behind me, her hands over her face.

"Go to the kitchen," I said, jostling her foot with mine, trying to rouse her. "Bring us some water."

She sniffled and looked around, and seemed surprised to realize her employer was no longer with us in the hallway. Quickly, she got to her feet and rushed from the hallway. I had no idea whether she'd return with water or not.

As soon as we were alone, I dropped to Achilles' side. "Why are you here?"

"Why are you?" he asked, his eyes accusatory. "Rose told you to stay away."

"And I'm sure she'll be glad I didn't, given what just happened." I gestured to his face and the ruined chair at his feet. "You were nearly killed."

"I would have fought him off," he said. "I'd been awake for a few minutes before you arrived. I was feigning sleep, waiting for the right moment to attack him."

"Did he do that to your eye?" The lump next to Achilles' eye was swollen and painful looking.

He shrugged. "Whoever did it snuck up on me while I was still outside. I didn't see, but considering no one else has rushed in to attack us, I assume it was Alexander. Whoever it was, it hurts like the devil."

He pressed a hand to the floor and began trying to stand up.

"Wait, you aren't ready. We need to—"

"Stay here and wait for him and his helpers to return?" Achilles asked. He shook his head. "No, we need to go. We need to alert the authorities. I should have done it before I arrived, but I wasn't certain."

"Certain of what?"

He stood up and braced himself against the wall, blinking to clear his vision. "Of his true identity. I had my suspicions, but I needed to be sure before I told Rose. Though, if we are being honest, I think she already knows."

"I think so, too," I admitted.

Achilles extended an elbow to me, and I took it for what it was: his way of asking for help. I wrapped my hand around his arm and allowed him to rest against me as we moved down the hallway. He needed to see a doctor about his head. The bruise on his temple was significant enough that he should probably have been lying down, but he was right. There was no time for resting. Not here, anyway.

Halfway down the hallway, he stooped to pick up the gun I'd stolen from Walter and tucked it in the back of his waistband beneath his jacket. It wasn't loaded, but there was no need to leave a perfectly good weapon lying on the floor where anyone could find it.

I helped him down the stairs, moving slowly, giving him a second after each step to steady himself lest we both go tumbling headlong down them.

"I thought The Chess Master might be behind the art thefts here as soon as we were contacted by the museum," Achilles continued. "It looked so much like the thefts he had committed in London. Then, I learned of Alexander Lockwell, and the name sounded familiar."

"Had he used the identity before?"

Achilles shook his head. "Not quite, but he went by Augustus Lockwood in London."

I laughed bitterly. The similarities were undeniable. "He was practically begging someone to notice."

"What's the point in a life of crime if there is no one chasing you?" Achilles asked. "That is what The Chess Master lives for—the game. Rose tried her best not to play. She didn't want to believe it could be him, so I had to investigate it on my own."

"You didn't have to," I said. "You could have asked me."

He snorted. "Rose would have killed me herself if I'd done such a thing."

"I'm an adult. She can't stop me from making my own choices."

"But I'm her husband," he said. "She can keep me from making mine. I had to do it alone, I'm sorry. Though, I'm more than grateful you are here now. Had he not been outnumbered, I'm not sure he would have run off the way he did."

The maid was waiting at the bottom of the stairs with a glass of water and a cold compress. She gave both to Achilles, and he drank the glass and pressed the compress to his forehead with a wince.

I handed her the empty glass and touched her shoulder. "I'd suggest you vacate the premises immediately. By the looks of it, you were surprised by the extent of your employer's crimes. Let me assure you, they are far greater than what you saw. You won't be safe here."

Her eyes went wide, and I nodded, staring back at her,

hoping I was conveying the full extent of the danger she was in.

"And if you weren't surprised," Achilles added. "Use this opportunity to find a more noble line of work. Leave now and alert the police immediately. Unless you want to be viewed as an accomplice, you should turn him in."

When we made it outside, the sky had turned dark, the clouds hanging heavily over us, threatening rain any second. I ran around the side of the house and grabbed Achilles' cane. He looked relieved to see his old friend again and took it gratefully, resting his weight on it at once.

"Do you think we should still alert the police to the crime ourselves?" I asked. "I'm not sure we can trust the maid. She looked petrified. Even if she isn't part of his plans, I'm not sure she'll actually go to the police."

"Her being petrified is the reason I know she will," he said. "She was frightened and needed something tangible to do. So, I gave it to her. Anyway, she seemed by nature to be easily frightened, so the idea of prison will terrify her to the core. She'll do whatever she can to ensure that doesn't happen."

I smiled up at him, amazed once again at his ability to read and understand people. Suddenly, he froze and turned to me, his thin mustache twitching in thought. "Wait a second. Alice, where did you come from? Why were you here?"

I'd been so invested in Achilles' story that I'd nearly forgotten my own. "Oh, yes. One of Alexander's associates attempted to kidnap me."

Monsieur Prideaux's eyes went wide, but I waved away his worry. "The man is currently trapped in a wooden crate at a warehouse by the docks. He intended to hand me over to Alexander in order to barter for his own freedom."

"We have to go there at once," Achilles said, grabbing my arm and pulling me towards the street, his other hand waving for a car.

"Go where?" I asked. "The warehouse? Believe me, Walter Miller deserves a few more hours trapped in a box. I'm more than happy to send the police to fetch him."

"It is where The Chess Master will go," he said. "Or, it's the most likely place, anyway. Since he ran from the house, he'll need supplies before he can escape again. Given the fact he was able to jump over a bridge into the Thames and survive it, I'm certain he has backup plans hidden all over this city. One of which is probably hidden at the warehouse."

A cab stopped in front of us, and Achilles opened the door and turned back to me, eyebrows raised, silently asking whether I was coming along.

I'd had more than enough adventure for one day, but none of it would be worth anything if The Chess Master wasn't caught.

"That seems like it is worth a try," I said with a shrug.

Since I didn't know the address, I directed the cab driver to the general area of the warehouse. On the drive, the sky began to spit and eventually grew to a full rain. Water slicked over the roads and filled the gutters, slowing our progress across town. I wanted to beg the driver to speed up, but I also knew a car accident would only slow us down further.

Finally, we arrived, but the rain was coming down too

hard to be certain which warehouse was the correct one, so I had the driver weave back and forth through the narrow streets and alleys until I saw the one I believed belonged to The Chess Master.

"Are you sure this is the place?" the driver asked, looking over his shoulder to take in our appearance. We were both dressed in fine clothes that signified our station in society—a station that wouldn't naturally place us at an old warehouse near the docks in the evening—but Achilles also had an ever-growing bruise that had all but swollen his eye shut.

I squinted towards the building and then turned towards Achilles. "I think so. Walter's driver isn't here anymore, but I think this is it."

That was enough for Achilles. He shrugged and then climbed out of the car and, ever the gentleman, offered me a hand.

Before accepting his offer, I asked the driver if he could send word to the police to meet us at the warehouse immediately. He narrowed his eyes at me, but when Achilles increased the fare to nearly double what it had been, the driver agreed. He took Achilles' money and left immediately, not caring to stick around and see what trouble we were getting into at the warehouse. I admired him. If I were a bit less curious, I'd find myself in far fewer life or death situations.

Achilles lifted an arm to shield his eyes from the rain and looked at the warehouse. "It doesn't seem like anyone is here."

"We won't know until we try." I waved him on and walked ahead, doing my best to pretend I wasn't terrified.

"Do you want to wait for the police?" he asked. "It could be dangerous."

"Waiting could be dangerous, too," I said. "Not for us, but for the general public. If Alexander escapes, he will kill again."

We both knew the stakes—life or death—but we both also understood that protecting the world from the likes of The Chess Master was more important than our individual lives. If he was inside, preparing to disappear into the storm only to pop up somewhere else in a few months, we had to do our best to stop him.

I led Achilles around the side of the warehouse to the door Walter had taken me through. The chain that had been used to lock the door was lying on the ground and the door was partially open. I peeked through it to the dark warehouse beyond, and then pushed the door in. When nothing immediately happened, I stepped inside.

Achilles followed and then positioned himself in front of me, doing his best to shield me from the unknown threat. Then, we heard the muffled sounds of screaming.

Achilles jumped, but I grabbed his arm and pointed towards the crate where I'd left Walter a few hours before. "It's the man I trapped. He's in there."

Another scream broke through, but this time, I gasped.

It was not the scream of a man, but a woman.

Achilles reached the same realization I had and rushed forward, sliding the crate on top to the side as though it was nothing and pulling back the lid. As soon as the lid was open, he dropped to his knees.

"Rose?" His voice sounded strangled as he reached

into the crate and helped a woman out of the box. His wife.

Her blonde hair was stuck through with straw and bits of paper, and tear tracks ran down her cheeks, ruining the makeup she wore to hide an old scar that had faded over the years but that still stood out in the right lighting.

"What happened to you?" Achilles asked.

At the same time, Rose looked between us. "How are you here? How did you find me?"

"So many questions and so little time," a now familiar voice said from over my shoulder.

Rose clapped a hand over her mouth and gasped just as I felt the thin edge of a knife kiss the skin of my neck. I didn't need to turn around to know Alexander Lockwell was standing behind me. It was just as well I didn't because, with the way he had the knife pressed to my neck, I couldn't move at all. Even breathing felt danger-ous. With every pulse of my heart, my neck pressed a bit harder against the blade.

"I was supposed to be leaving now." The Chess Master sounded frustrated. He let out a long sigh, his breath warm against the back of my neck. "But you all cannot let me go in peace."

"Put the knife down, Jimmy," Achilles said, using The Chess Master's true name. He grabbed Rose's arm and pulled her close to his side, tucking her partially behind him, shielding her body with his. "You don't need to hurt anyone."

"Well running away isn't doing me any favors," Alexander said. "You keep showing up again. How am I meant to be rid of you if I don't kill you?"

Rose poked her head out from behind Achilles' shoulder. "You could fake your own death, brother. That worked last time."

"But only for a short while," Alexander said, sounding truly disappointed. "After my planned jump from the bridge into the Thames, I thought I'd shaken you for sure. I received word you were in the city last week, but my operation has so many layers now, I didn't believe you would ever connect the missing art back to me. Even if you managed to arrest some of my associates, my name would never slip from between their lips. I made sure of that."

"Blackmail?" Rose asked. "Did you threaten their friends? Their families?"

The Chess Master chuckled, amused by his own schemes. "What else is stronger than the bonds of family? People tie themselves to one another emotionally and make themselves weak. I do not feel guilty about using those connections for my own gain."

"I don't believe you are capable of feeling guilt about anything anymore," Rose said.

"Are you judging me?" he demanded. "You, who allowed your foolish cousin to become involved even after what happened to the last one?"

The last one.

Edward.

"You ordered my brother murdered?" I asked. I already knew the answer but for some reason I needed to hear him say it.

"Of course I did, silly girl," Alexander whispered in my ear. "He was caught in his own crime and attempted to blame me. Rather than suffer the consequences of his incompetence, he wanted to lighten his sentence by having me arrested. I had no choice."

"There's always a choice."

He laughed. "Yes, and I chose the better option. I was not going to hang for the likes of your brother."

"What about the likes of me?" Rose asked.

I felt The Chess Master shift behind me to look up at his sister. She'd been hiding behind Achilles, but now she'd stepped forward, facing him with no one and nothing between them.

"Would you kill me to save yourself, too?" she asked.

"I don't want to," he admitted. "It is why I jumped from the bridge that day years ago. I wanted life to be easier for you. You'd found this family who loved you, and we never had that growing up. Not really. I didn't want to ruin things for you, and I figured it would be easier if I was dead."

"Don't pretend your motives were so pure," Rose said, shaking her head. "You wanted to avoid being arrested."

"And I found a solution that accomplished both things. That isn't wrong; it's clever."

"Not clever enough, unfortunately," Rose said.

"Unfortunately," Alexander repeated. "Now, you've left me no other choice."

The knife pressed more firmly against my neck, and I whimpered, straining up onto my toes to try and get away from the blade. He'd spent so long talking with Rose that I'd fooled myself into thinking maybe The Chess Master had forgotten about me. But now, the reality was hard and cold against my neck. He was going to kill me.

"You can't kill us all," Achilles said. His eye was a mass of purple and black now, but he seemed steadier on his feet. Certainly more able to fight than he had been before. He was right. With Achilles and Rose, Alexander wouldn't be able to hold them both back.

"But I can cut her throat," Alexander said, gripping my arm more tightly and pulling me back against him. "And I know neither of you will leave her to die alone in this warehouse while you chase after me. You'll stay and render her aid, and by the time she is dead, I'll be gone."

His words sent a shiver down my spine because...he was right.

The story would play out exactly as he'd said. Rose and Achilles would never leave me to die in this warehouse. They would stay with me, and in that time, Alexander would disappear and reappear somewhere else under another alias. I would die and it would all be for nothing.

There would be no justice for Edward. No justice for Helen. No justice for the countless other men and women who had been victimized by The Chess Master.

More than that, there would be no justice for his future victims. More people would be ensnared in his web, and he would carry on manipulating people for his own purposes with no consequences.

"Don't save me," I said all at once. Tears burned in the backs of my eyes, but I looked towards the warehouse's exposed ceiling, trying to hold them back. "Follow him and end this."

Achilles shook his head and looked from his wife to The Chess Master and back again, waiting for her to say something. His good eye was wide and pleading, but Rose just stared past me blankly, looking at her brother.

"She won't," Alexander said, quietly enough that it

felt like he was talking only to me. I didn't know whether Rose and Achilles could hear him or not. "My sister pretends otherwise, but she doesn't want to capture me. I'm the only family she has left, no offense to you and your parents, of course."

I wanted to tell him he was wrong, but Rose had been resistant to me looking for The Chess Master. She didn't want to engage with him again, and I'd assumed it was because she thought he was too dangerous, but perhaps her motives had more to do with him being her family than anything else. Perhaps, she didn't want to be the one to ruin her own brother.

In a way, I could understand it.

Edward had done terrible things to land himself in prison. If I'd known about them before the police, would I have turned him in? I liked to believe so, but I would never truly know.

Was Rose a better person than I was? Would she seek justice always, even to the detriment of her only remaining family?

"Well, Rose," The Chess Master said, stepping to the side slightly, tightening his grip on the knife. "This is goodbye."

I closed my eyes.

As the end came for me, death seemed such a certainty that I didn't grab for the blade or fight back. Instead, I simply waited for the end.

The blade was repositioned on the left side of my neck, the tip pressing into my skin, and I knew its cut would be deep and true. If anyone knew how to properly slit a throat, it would be a man like The Chess Master.

Someone who had the blood of countless others on his hands. There would be no saving me from my wounds.

I felt his breath hot against the side of my face, and the sound of my own pulse in my ears washed out everything else. It drowned out the sound of Achilles shouting and Rose begging for my life. The thudding of my heartbeat, pounding away in my chest, was loud enough that for a moment, I didn't even register the gunshot.

I didn't understand that anything had happened until a warm, heavy mass fell against my shoulder and then slid to the floor.

I opened my eyes and sobbed when I saw the body at my feet.

The Chess Master. Dead.

Rose was still holding a gun, the end smoking from the bullet she'd fired, and she was blinking at the space where, a moment before, her brother had been standing.

I backed away as blood puddled around his head, spreading outward quickly. I kept walking backwards until my back hit the metal wall of the warehouse and I had nowhere else to go.

Then, I slid to the ground, cupped my hands over my face, and wept.

16

R ose had shot and killed her own brother, yet I was the one who couldn't stop weeping.

Rose held and comforted me as I explained everything to her. I told her about my encounter with Walter Miller and how Achilles and I had pursued The Chess Master from his home to the warehouse. In return, she described to me how she had followed up on a sudden lead in the art theft investigation that had led her to the warehouse at exactly the right time. We talked until the police arrived, which didn't take too long. Apparently, the cab driver didn't simply take Achilles' money and leave. He actually sent the police to us.

Achilles knew the officers from the work he and Rose had been doing for the museum, so he walked them through the afternoon and the events that led to the scene before them: a dead man and a weeping woman.

Naturally, he left out the part about his wife being the dead man's sister. According to Rose's feelings on the matter, Nellie Dennet hadn't been her identity for years. She was as much Rose Beckingham as she was the orphaned girl from Five Points, New York.

"What of Walter Miller? Where is he now?" I asked, wiping the tears from my face. I felt foolish crying in front of so many people, but I couldn't seem to stop the flow of tears no matter how hard I tried.

"It's shock," Rose said, without answering my question. "You've been through a lot today."

So had Rose. She'd been trapped in a crate and was forced to kill her own brother to save me, yet she wasn't weeping. In a quiet moment while Rose was talking with the officers, Achilles assured me Rose would cry later.

"She doesn't like to cry in front of other people," he said. "But she will. Don't you worry, she will."

"Walter Miller?" I overheard an officer ask.

Rose nodded. "It is the man you're thinking of, I'm sure. He worked at the museum and even helped early on in the investigation into the thefts. As my cousin uncovered, however, he was a key player in Alexander Lockwell's plan, and he attempted to kidnap my cousin earlier today."

"Where is he now?" the officer asked, looking around the warehouse. The entire building had been searched from top to bottom. The art in the crates was cataloged and weapons were collected, as well as anything that could be used as evidence that Alexander Lockwell was Augustus Lockwood, who was The Chess Master. So, I knew without a doubt that Walter Miller was long gone.

"I was knocked unconscious before being put into the crate," Rose explained. "But since my cousin was able to put Walter in that very same crate earlier this afternoon, I have to assume Walter was freed by The Chess Master."

"If he's smart, he is hiding," Achilles said.

"Wherever he is, we'll find him," the officer said, giving me an encouraging smile. "He won't get away."

We stayed until Alexander Lockwell's body was carried away. I couldn't say why, but it was important for me to see him actually be loaded into a coroner's vehicle and taken away. I needed to see that he was dead, though the bullet to his head should have been more than enough proof.

Once his body was gone, I allowed Achilles and Rose to escort me to a car and take me home.

Aunt Sarah fussed over all of us into the night and all the next day. She blamed herself for not helping Rose send me away when she tried.

"I'm a foolish old woman," she said, cupping her face in her hands and shaking her head. "I was lonely and allowed that loneliness to make me selfish. I should have never let you come here, Alice."

"If she hadn't, I might very well be dead," Achilles said.

The day before, he'd sworn he would have fought his way out of The Chess Master's grasp, but distance from the event—and the worsening discoloration of the bruise around his eye—seemed to change his tune.

"Don't say that," Rose begged him.

"It's true," he insisted. "Alice saved my life, and I will

forever be grateful that she came to New York and wasn't sent away."

Rose elbowed him in the side. "Don't encourage her."

I was glad to know Achilles valued my presence, but I didn't like seeing myself as a hero. As far as investigations went, mine had mostly been a failure. My instincts had been good, but my attempts at gathering information nearly saw me kidnapped and killed by one of the most powerful men in New York City. Without Rose and Achilles, I would be dead. In truth, we all relied heavily on one another.

"Wait," I said, holding up a hand to get their attention, and turning to Rose. "How did you procure a gun?"

"What?" Rose asked.

"At the warehouse. You were in the crate, and Achilles helped you out, and then you found a gun to shoot and..." My voice trailed off. Rose hadn't shown any outward signs of distress or regret in regards to the killing of her brother, but I still felt uncomfortable broaching the subject directly.

She hooked a thumb over her shoulder, pointing at her husband who was inspecting his eye in a mirror above Aunt Sarah's fireplace. "Achilles had a weapon tucked into the back of his trousers.

"But there were no bullets," I said. "I fired it back at the house and—"

Achilles said. "The gun malfunctioned when you attempted to shoot Alexander, but it remained loaded."

I frowned, imagining what could have been if I'd known what I was doing. I'd never been trained to use a weapon, so I had simply pulled the trigger and hoped for the best. How would things have gone differently if I could have shot and killed Alexander back at his house?

"So, Achilles pulled me out of the box, pushed me behind him, and then lifted the back of his coat to reveal the gun. I cleared the jam and was able to use the weapon."

I'd thought it was strange that Rose had allowed herself to be protected behind Achilles, but now it all made sense. It had been a rouse to give her the privacy necessary to ready the weapon.

I shook my head. "I could have done that at the house if I'd known. I'm sorry, Rose."

Rose stood up and crossed the room. "You have nothing to be sorry for, Alice. I'm glad it was me."

"You can't mean that."

She cut me off with a quick wave. "I do. I'm glad it was me. I know Jimmy hurt your brother and your family, and I will always be sorry for that, but I would be even sorrier if you had to carry the guilt of killing my brother around for the rest of your life."

My heart clenched at her words. "I hadn't thought of it like that."

Killing The Chess Master would have felt like revenge in the moment, but it would have been bittersweet later. Knowing that I took away Rose's last living family member out of anger for my brother would have eaten away at me.

Almost as if she could read my thoughts, Rose wrapped an arm around my shoulders and pulled me close. "You are my family, Alice. You and Catherine and your parents."

"And me," Achilles said, winking at his wife.

She rolled her eyes at him but had to fight back a smile. Then, she sobered and turned back to me. "You were right at the beginning, Alice. I was trying to protect my brother. Not because he deserved to be protected, but because I didn't want to be the one to capture him. I didn't want to be the reason he was hanged or spent his life in prison. I didn't want him to hold that over me, and I didn't want to hold it over myself. But the moment he threatened your life, my decision was obvious. Given the choice over and over again, I would choose to save you."

And again, I wept.

I hugged Rose and cried tears of gratitude into her shoulder. I felt foolish and emotional, but I also felt love. Familial love for my wonderful cousin.

ROSE AND ACHILLES left a week later.

Aunt Sarah and I saw them to the train station. Rose invited Aunt Sarah out to see them in San Francisco, and she promised she would write to me more. Achilles remained quiet and stoic, only breaking once to pull me into a bone crushing hug before boarding the train. We waved to them from the station until the train was out of view, and then Aunt Sarah and I walked back to the car together, planning what we would eat for lunch.

The art from the warehouse was inspected and returned to the museum with the exhibition scheduled to open at the end of the week and remain open for a year. The museum expected it to be one of their most popular exhibitions ever after the story of The Chess Master's capture ran in newspapers around the globe.

Rose tried to convince me to take my credit for his capture, but I was more than happy to let all of the praise land on Rose and Achilles. Their private detective business would boom on account of the publicity, and besides, I didn't particularly want to talk about The Chess Master. With the public or the press. I'd come far too close to losing everything, and I'd rather separate myself from it as much as possible.

My contribution was included in a small way, though. The article described a "helpful witness" who showed Achilles to the warehouse and distracted The Chess Master, allowing Rose to shoot him dead. That was more than enough recognition for me.

"Now that it is safe, you are free to stay with me as long as you like," Aunt Sarah said over breakfast one day. "I know I'm a boring old woman, but I think having you young people around keeps me interesting."

"You are already interesting," I promised her.

I had been considering lengthening my stay. I enjoyed spending time with Aunt Sarah, and I'd been so consumed with the investigation that I hadn't seen much of the city.

Still, the deaths of Helen and The Chess Master hung heavily over my head, like a perpetual rain cloud dampening the fun. I wasn't sure I'd be able to shake them until I was on a boat and headed for home.

"I'm not sure when I'll leave, but I'll be here today," I said, sounding as chipper as I could muster. "Would you like to go to lunch?"

Aunt Sarah suddenly became very interested in her plate. She pushed cut fruit around with her fork, and I thought I noticed her cheeks turn a darker shade of pink.

"I can't today. Maybe tomorrow?"

"All right," I agreed, eyes narrowing in suspicion. "What do you have planned today?"

"Just lunch." She waved it away as though it was nothing, but I had never seen my very confident aunt so nervous. Then, I noticed the color on her eyelids and remembered the unusual scent of perfume I'd smelled when she'd hugged me.

"Just lunch?" I asked, eyebrow raised. "Would your companion for lunch happen to be of the male persuasion?"

Her cheeks flared, and I slapped my hand on the table. "I knew it. You have a romantic engagement, Aunt Sarah!"

She shushed me, but I was too giddy to be quiet.

"With who?"

She shook her head, but I refused to relent until she told me.

"My butcher," she said, covering her face with her hands.

My jaw fell open. "Marco?"

"I've been going in to see him once a week for months, and he finally asked to see me outside of my weekly trip for meat." She lowered her hands, her face flaming red, and tried to take a sip of her water, but she lowered her glass before it even reached her lips. "Am I foolish? Suppose people find out? The difference in our classes alone will make me the scandal of society. Anyway, I've been widowed for twenty years. I shouldn't be seeing my butcher. It is—"

"Wonderful," I finished for her, banishing any other negative word she might want to replace it with. "It is wonderful, Aunt Sarah. Everyone in the family will be happy to know that you aren't alone in the city anymore."

Her eyes went wide, and she pointed a stern finger at me. "No one else in the family must know. Do you hear me, Alice? This is our secret."

I held up a hand and made her a solemn vow. "No one will know of you and Marco until you wish for them to."

Aunt Sarah must have believed me because she relaxed through the rest of breakfast and then stopped by my room to have me wish her luck before Marco arrived to collect her.

"You'll have a wonderful time," I assured her. "If he doesn't fall madly in love with you, he is the most foolish man in existence."

She rolled her eyes, but looked to be standing a bit taller than she had when she'd first walked into the room.

"Oh," she said, reaching into her pocket and pulling out two squares of paper. "These came for you this afternoon. One is a telegram from Catherine and the other is a letter with no return address. Despite my curiosity, I didn't read either."

"Good. If you had, I would have been forced to tell Catherine all about your butcher."

"Wicked girl," Aunt Sarah teased.

I took the letters from her, gave her a final wave, and then dropped onto my bed and tore into the unaddressed letter.

Alice,

First, I'm not sorry.
> *You always find some reason to be cross with me, and*

most of the time, your reasons are justified. On this occasion, however, your reasons are rubbish.

I warned you to keep away from The Chess Master, not because I do not think you are capable, but because I care for your safety. Caring for you does not make me a bad man —though it might make me very foolish. I stand by my warnings and hope this letter finds you safely in New York.

Second, I miss you.

Regardless of whether you believe our relationship is more business than personal, I miss talking with you. Life is more interesting with you in it, and I hope you will be in mine again soon.

Yours,

Sherborne Sharp.

He'd sent it only a few days after I'd left. Meaning, he'd missed me within the first week.

I read the letter twice over, smiling the entire time.

Each time Aunt Sarah had pressed me to stay in New York, Sherborne Sharp's face had appeared in my mind. I'd done my best to ignore it, but now that I'd read his letter and knew the contents of his heart, I didn't think I'd be able to ignore it any longer.

I was reading the letter through a third time when I remembered Catherine's telegram.

Likely, she was writing back to me in regards to the death of her friend Helen Davis, so I was not eager to read her telegram and so quickly lose the good feelings Sherborne's letter had brought. Still, I read it out of a sense of duty.

Alice. Come to Yorkshire immediately. Speak to no one. The matter is urgent.

It was surprisingly little information, but I could feel Catherine's desperation. Something must be very wrong for her to have contacted me in this way. I read the brief lines again, hoping to find a hint as to the cause of her concern buried there, but there was nothing. Just a plea for me to come to Yorkshire right away.

I'd been debating how long I would stay in New York, and then Sherborne's letter had made me long for London. Now, however, the only place in the world I wanted to be was in Yorkshire with my sister. Her telegram had left me with a sinking feeling in my stomach, a premonition that some sort of darkness hovered over her.

I tucked both letters into my pocket and began packing my things at once.

Continue following the mysterious adventures of Alice Beckingham in "Murder by Twilight."

ABOUT THE AUTHOR

Blythe Baker is the lead writer behind several popular historical and paranormal mystery series. When Blythe isn't buried under clues, suspects, and motives, she's acting as chauffeur to her children and head groomer to her household of beloved pets. She enjoys walking her dog, lounging in her backyard hammock, and fiddling with graphic design. She also likes binge-watching mystery shows on TV.

To learn more about Blythe, visit her website and sign up for her newsletter at www.blythebaker.com